D1333412

AS RICH AS THE KING

'With this book, Abigail Assor announces herself as one of the most distinctive voices in North African literature. This is a vibrant, sensual, subversive novel with an unforgettable heroine'

LEÏLA SLIMANI

'Abigail Assor's writing is precise, sensual, subversive and wildly lyrical. Astonishing'

LE PARISIEN

'The shooting star of French literature… Her style is powerful, poetic, precise, clever and rousing. Whoever can write like this, without affect, drama, acrobatics or tricks is a great writer'

KULTUR & SERVICE

'Stunning in its truth, cruelty and style'

PARIS MATCH

AS RICH AS THE KING

TRANSLATED FROM
THE FRENCH BY
NATASHA LEHRER

PUSHKIN PRESS

ABIGAIL ASSOR

Pushkin Press
Somerset House, Strand
London WC2R ILA

As Rich as the King was first published as *Aussi riche que le roi* by Gallimard in Paris, 2021

First published by Pushkin Press in 2023

This book is supported by the Institut Français (Royaume-Uni) as part of the Burgess Programme.

ROYAUME-UNI

1 3 5 7 9 8 6 4 2

ISBN 13: 978-1-78227-890-0

Designed and typeset by Tetragon, London
Printed and bound by Clays Ltd, Elcograf S.p.A.

www.pushkinpress.com

AS RICH AS THE KING

I

ONCE A BOY TOLD HER that in other places, far away, the sand was velvety soft, white as clouds. He talked about seashells and the smell of salt, the music of the waves. She didn't believe him. Those kids from the Carrières Centrales, they're always telling stories to bewitch you, the jerks. Here, beneath her, the sand was yellow and grey; it smelt of stubbed-out cigarettes, and if she rubbed against it, it nicked her skin. It was gross, but that's what it was like, Casablanca sand. At least it was real.

They must have been asleep in the sun for three hours by then. At least the Casablanca sun never disappoints—every time, it's like drowning in light, it cloaks you, envelops you, melts you up entirely. Maybe, lying there together, they'd die, melt away, vanish, one by one they'd turn into slimy globules of fat, and when their parents came looking for them, when they got to Beach 56 they'd just find a big, murky, greenish puddle, they wouldn't even know the puddle was their children's melted bodies. Well, the others' parents probably wouldn't even bother to come looking for them, they were twenty-three. But her mother would come to find her, definitely.

She couldn't tell anymore where their bodies began and ended, where the limits of her skin were; there were legs, hot and weltering, all the grains of sand, the corner of a rough towel, her nose in someone's arm. Everyone dozing, and the footballs bouncing in the water and splashing everyone, the sound of kids yelling in the streets, the shriek of car horns on the avenue behind them, none of it mattered—the sounds of life, as Yaya liked to say. Reminding us we're not dead.

Eventually, slowly, everyone began to uncouple. From the shapeless mass, one after another, bodies unravelled; it was like a dance—not a dance from here, a modern dance from France. The boys clasped their legs between their arms and the girls lay on their stomachs, bending their legs like little Lolitas. Sarah didn't pose like that. She sat with the boys. They chatted a bit, drank some expensive Sidi Ali water, agreed that actually it had a bit of a sour tang. Yaya threw stones into the Atlantic, he said one day he'd end up killing a seagull, not on purpose, it would be the seagull's fault, because it should have known Yaya threw stones into the Atlantic at that exact spot every day. He was right, Sarah thought. The thing that got on her nerves was the way Driss didn't look at her at all. He was acting like he used to six months ago, the bastard, like he used to before the whole thing started. All the boys looked at her, even the really angry ones, even after she'd told them the most terrible lies, they all carried on looking at her. That guy from La Notte, when he found out she was only sixteen, he kept on looking at her—he looked at her even more. But Driss sat there with his notebook writing down bullshit and getting sand everywhere like he didn't give a damn about her. He wasn't even good-looking. He was pretty ugly, actually.

'Fuck's sake, is he ever going to give up?' It was Chirine who spoke, still lying on her front like an American starlet. A street kid was trying to sell her a black-market cigarette or a piece of Flash Wondermint chewing gum. They could be really insistent, those little urchins. They'd be like, 'Flash Wondermint, please, madame, Flash Wondermint, please.' They always spoke in French because it made them look polite.

'What's the problem, Chirine?' said Alain.

'That brat's asked me ten times.'

'He's annoying you?'

'Yeah. Ten times.'

Alain got up and went towards the kid. He couldn't have been more than fourteen, skinny, with blemishes on his dark skin.

'Hey, kid, what's your name?' asked Alain in Arabic.

'Abdellah.'

'Abdellah. Abdellah, my girlfriend has told you ten times to get lost. You leave her alone, all right?'

'But monsieur, just one cigarette, monsieur, just one, please.'

'You see? He's a nightmare,' Chirine said.

'What about a chewing gum, monsieur, please.'

Alain patted the kid gently on the back and told him to get going, coaxing him in the direction of the road. But the kid was going nowhere. His threadbare trainers planted in the sand, he was wired, a warrior, ready to fight. He kept saying, 'One cigarette, please, monsieur, one cigarette,' his voice beseeching, but there was nothing beseeching in his eyes. His eyes were full of fight.

'Just ignore him,' said Chirine, but before she finished speaking, something came flying through the air, swift and violent, and hit the kid on the arm; scared, he ran off.

It was Badr. He'd thrown his shoe.

'Good riddance,' he said.

They went back to their lazing, skin sweaty and sticky, dozing on and off, laughing. A few hours later the sun began to go down, it was time to go. Sarah pulled on her dress and flip-flops, and they all walked towards the main avenue filled with the roar of traffic and hawkers selling corn on the cob. They kissed each other goodbye, and when she embraced Driss she tried to give him a lingering kiss on the cheek that would mean something, make him understand. It didn't work. The second she'd finished pressing her lips to his skin he turned to the road without a word, eyes fixed to the ground, and walked towards the carpark behind McDonald's, where he'd left his motorbike.

The others were leaving too, everyone heading in different directions. Sarah made as if she was going north, towards Anfa Supérieur, where the beautiful villas basked, but she soon turned east towards Hay Mohammadi. She walked for nearly an hour. It was dark by the time she reached home.

Home was a falling-down brick building. There was never any hot water. Since there were no curtains or shutters on the windows, she could see from the street that the lights were out, that her mother wasn't back. Further along on the right, behind some rusty fencing, loomed the bidonville. There the shacks were built of old flattened petrol cans, and all around you could see the names and colours of service stations, Afriquia, Mobil, Total. At least her house was made of brick, thought Sarah, and even if they weren't amazing bricks, and it was damp, it wasn't so bad; her mother always said that so long as you're on the right side of the tracks, you're not on the wrong side of the tracks.

She was about to open the front door when she heard a voice—she knew he'd be here, the little shit.

'Sarah! Sarah!' Without turning round, she said in Arabic, 'Sorry, but honestly you deserved it.' He chuckled. On the other side of the fencing, Abdellah balanced like a monkey on some railings. 'You think you're better than we are, Lalla Sarah, because you hang out with the rich kids?'

He was always coming out with this thing about the rich kids. It made him laugh to call her Lalla, giving her a swanky title because he thought she fancied herself a queen. But she knew one day she really would be addressed as Lalla, and the little Arab brat would still be stuck in this slum.

'Of course I'm better than you. I'm French. We're not the same, idiot.'

As she went inside, she distinctly heard Abdellah hiss, 'We're exactly the same.'

2

Six months earlier

D RISS HAD THIS WAY of not looking at girls. The very first time she ever saw him, at the beginning of 1994, his eyes had slid right over her. As if she'd been a current of air—there was nothing about her that caught his eye. Suddenly she was a little girl again, sneaking snake-like into the Lynx cinema on Avenue Mers Sultan. She'd plunge her entire being into the dark pupils of the Egyptian stars; and those beautiful Cairene eyes, staring straight out of the screen, gave her nothing back. They too slid right over her.

That day, six months before Beach 56, before it all kicked off, she was with Kamil at the Campus, the café opposite the lycée's Building K, the one where the rich kids, pretty girls and boys in leather jackets, hung out. A bit further down, there was a pool café she sometimes went to. As well as shooting pool, you could smoke whatever you wanted there and eat the tuna and tomato sauce sandwich that you'd got on credit from Moustache, the old guy at the shop on the next street.

But she'd never have admitted to Kamil that she went to the pool café. He'd held the door open a little for her as they went into Café Campus, and she listened to him tell her he worked in telecoms with his father. Which meant whatever it meant.

He wasn't bad-looking, Kamil, not exactly good-looking either, and she liked that. She sometimes thought he went on a bit about his car and his fancy pad in a swanky neighbourhood where everyone went to play cards in the evening; but for that kind of a guy, he could have been a lot worse. He watched her from behind his black coffee and banana split. He seemed astonished, she could feel every feature of her face fluttering towards him. Her long, straight nose, he saw it, loved it, the same for her dark skin and princess eyes that stretched towards her temples. All of it, he loved it all, wanted to possess it all. This was the third time he'd brought her to the café. Sarah had figured out the technique the year before. To wait before she took off her clothes. It worked. Boys were such fools, they'd buy you endless coffees to get a result. And sometimes they kept it up afterwards, when they thought they were in love. Kamil was the worst, they hadn't even kissed yet. She thought it was sweet.

He talked non-stop. 'My villa in Dar Bouazza, five bedrooms, six bathrooms, I'll take you there sometime if you like,' he said. 'It's not bad in Casa, it's true, but what I want to see is America, the other side of the Atlantic. You realize, right,' he said, 'when we're on Beach 56, on the other side of the ocean it's America? I'll take you there—hey, why are you laughing, I'm serious, I'm telling you.'

Sarah laughed anyway. She didn't doubt it for a moment. She laughed because suddenly he was very handsome, and she was even prettier, with him there on the other side of the water. She was wearing a broad-brimmed green hat, he had a moustache, they were strolling like aristocrats along a quayside, among a crowd of people hurrying towards the boats. Lightheaded and nervous, she laughed at these American beauties, because they were so beautiful it should be illegal. Kamil faltered, discouraged by her laughter, but Sarah said, 'No, tell me more.'

He started telling her about some hot and sticky New York nightclub, then he broke off suddenly.

'Hey, man!'

He'd caught sight of someone behind Sarah; she turned to see a young man taking off his motorcycle helmet, framed in the doorway. He had stocky, short legs and a little paunch. At Kamil's words he smiled, and little canine teeth appeared, smashed against thick gums, which folded under the shadow of a crooked nose, pointing to the ground. Yeah, pretty ugly.

Driss made his way over to them.

'Been a while, Driss! Your old man working you like a dog?'

'Not too bad, not too bad. How're you doing?'

Kamil prattled away about telecoms and America. And then Sarah saw the eyes. They were tiny but they were green, a complicated green, the green of the outdoors, nature, thyme leaves from the High Atlas, nothing like any eyes she'd ever seen—and this green slid right over her. Driss did not look at her once.

He turned to go, with a duck-footed gait that made his little belly wobble, and Kamil whispered, 'That guy is the richest of the rich. Richer than both of us. Maybe as rich as the king. But still, he's a good guy, you know.'

That was how it had begun: because Driss was rich. Richer than the lot of them, as rich as the king, richer than Kamil with his villa in Dar Bouazza. But maybe it was also because in his tiny green eyes there was thyme and bay, whose leaves she had seen melting into the beef tagines Loubna used to cook when she was a child. Loubna was her friend Séverine's au pair. She went there for lunch every Wednesday in the last year of primary school. Séverine used to call her the au pair rather than the maid, because she was polite, and she was French. And Sarah, with her mouth full and her teeth all greasy, would say, 'Me too, we have a Loubna too, at my house, with thyme leaves and beef and olives and cooking pots made of terracotta, like you. And we have gold and diamonds on the floor, and we trip over them, in my big house, like you do here.' It didn't matter if Séverine didn't believe her.

Yes, thyme certainly has its share of responsibility in this story. Later she wondered if it hadn't been for his eyes, and the way they brought back the tajine, Séverine, the last year of primary school, she might not have gone so far; she'd have picked another guy, also rich, maybe not as rich, but quite rich all the same. But the thing was, after that first encounter, she saw those eyes of thyme everywhere. In the café Kamil's face turned pale, grew wider, folded in on itself, until it morphed into Driss's face, with its crooked nose, its gums, its little canines, those eyes. It was as if it was Driss she'd been speaking to all along over the banana split at the Café Campus. When Kamil paid for her cinema ticket a few days later, it was Driss's hand she saw pulling apart the Velcro on his wallet, Driss's hand she felt gripping hers as they watched Amina Rachid being lectured on the big screen for having opened the door to the sheep delivery man with the sleeves of her djellaba rolled up. Kamil was licking an ice lolly and laughing at the husband's cries—'You show up naked like that even for the delivery man, and what am I, the fourth sheep?'—but it was Driss's laugh Sarah heard in the dark. The week after, it was as if she were playing cards with Driss in the villa in Dar Bouazza, and as if it was with Driss that she finally made love, praying it didn't sound the death knell of the Campus coffees, the cinema, the villa in Dar Bouazza. By the time she was fourteen, Sarah was going to bed with boys mainly for the paninis at lunch, but they always ended up spitting in her face a few days later with their friends in the school corridor, calling her a slut, and never paying for anything again. The girls talked about her too, with an air of disgust: 'She's not a virgin, the French girl. *C'est la hchouma.* Shameful.' Sarah didn't care, there were plenty of other rich guys in Casa, and plenty more paninis to be had. But every so often she didn't even get a panini out of it, and that was horrible. She learnt her lesson. By the time she was fifteen she'd changed her target: only older guys, at least nineteen, who'd left school already and had a fancy car. She'd pretend to be a shy little thing, madly in love, like the other girls; when they went to bed together, she'd say it was her first time. That worked better—even after she'd spent the night at Kamil's he didn't stop coming to pick her up from school and buying her lunch. In his open-top Porsche he told her he loved her, she held his hand. It smelt faintly of thyme.

People said Driss's father owned a Rolls Royce. She carved his name into the wood of the desks at school with the tip of her biro. At home, staring out of the window, she didn't see the laundry swaying or the boys sniffing glue. She saw, for the thousandth time, the movement of Driss's stubby legs as he climbed onto his motorbike. Richer than them all, as rich as the king; while she, instead of a helmet, placed a crown on her curly hair, a queen's crown, as rich as the queen.

3

THE GOOD THING about living next to the Carrières Centrales bidonville, rather than actually in it, was that you were a step closer to the west, to Anfa Supérieur, and so to America. Even if the gap spanned no more than the width of a fence, at least you were outside the slum, so it was like you'd almost escaped already. When Sarah saw Abdellah coming back from town lugging fifteen litres of water in plastic canisters bigger than he was, she rushed into the little kitchen, washed one of the two glasses and filled it with tap water. Then she went back outside and sat down nonchalantly on the front step, legs crossed, eyes closed, glass of water in hand, pretending to sunbathe. Abdellah was approaching the wire mesh fence now, panting, dragging the water canisters behind him, and when she heard him Sarah opened her eyes and mouth at the same time in her prettiest exclamation of surprise:

'Oh, hi, Abdellah! It's hot today, no?' Then, tilting her head and fluttering her eyelashes, she gave him her broadest American smile and took a sip from her glass. 'It's hot today, no?' was something actors said in the telenovelas that played on a loop at the pool café, and she thought it sounded cool. She'd stand front of the mirror in the girls' toilets at school, repeating it with different intonations, sometimes in an English accent, and using the stained towel that everyone used to dry their hands, but no one ever washed, to wipe her forehead. Sometimes the other girls watched her, sniggering, but Sarah didn't care. 'It's hot today, no, Abdellah?' It wasn't actually as hot as all that. Abdellah barely glanced at her through the fence as he dragged the canisters one by one to his door. Sarah carried on taking tiny sips from her glass. She waited till Abdellah had gone inside before spitting it out; no way was she really going to drink that foul water.

He was a right little bastard, Abdellah, even if he was kind of sweet too. He totally deserved her putting on a show like that. Once he'd said to her, 'Lalla Sarah, you're on the other side of the fence, and you really think you're outside? Maybe it's us who are outside and you're the one on the inside.' That was a really mean thing to say, the kind of thing that sticks to your skin and gets under your fingernails like dirt. Ever since then, at night, she sometimes had this dream of a stretch of sand in which she was swimming with a wire mesh over her mouth that let flurries of sand pour down her gagging throat, and she would try to scream, but the sand was inside her, and it was outside her too. Somewhere she could hear the sound of running water.

———

But a week after she saw Driss in the café, something happened—something to do with eyes, specifically eyes that are the colour of thyme and slide over girls. That was when Sarah knew she would never again have that dream at night, because soon she would only be drinking bottles of Sidi Ali water, and one day she was going to bathe in it, in a pale marble tub that could hold her a hundred times over, with a view onto a garden.

She was sitting in Kamil's convertible waiting for him outside the villa in Anfa Supérieur, when all of a sudden she heard the growl of a motorbike. She turned her head. She saw Driss behind her, he was looking from the numberplate to the villa and back. The fool took ages to notice her in the passenger seat. When he finally saw her, he lifted the visor on his helmet and called out in his reedy, high-pitched voice, 'Is this where Kamil lives?'

'Yeah,' she said.

'Tell him Driss says hi.' He started the engine and drove off.

But it didn't matter; those eyes of thyme and bay had seen her. Since that day in the Café Campus, all she'd been able to think about was him, with her by his side, the two of them raised up on brass platters borne by the outstretched arms of their servants beneath the night sky, dancing opposite each other to the rhythm of Arabic wedding songs and the adoring cries of the guests, stippled with light reflecting off the gold threads of her caftan and the rubies on her tiara. She saw herself stepping off the brass platter, and a maid, all dolled up for the occasion, wiping her forehead; Sarah would not thank her.

One morning, instead of going to school, she'd walked all the way to a little lane at the other end of Anfa, along the Rue de la Méditerranée—it was lined with hibiscus and waist-high hemlock, and trees that tilted towards each other until they touched, and when they touched they made a bridal canopy; she walked beneath it, slowly, unobserved. The days that followed, she made a list of the Rolexes he would give her—the same as the ones Kamil wore—and invented names for the gardeners she'd employ and get rid of according to her whim, with a click of her fingers. They'd fight to work for her, she'd pay so well. And then, at last, one warm January day, a little before noon, in front of Kamil's house, Driss's eyes darted towards her, and this time they didn't slide over her. Sarah knew that once a boy saw her, he could never take his eyes off her again.

She had this urge to go up to the fence, to call over to Abdellah and tell him, 'Abdellah, I don't care if I'm inside, if being inside means being surrounded by hibiscus trees in the greenery of Anfa, drinking Sidi Ali water you don't have to spit out, firing gardeners who aren't as poor as you, I don't care, I don't care if I'm inside.'

4

AT THE BEGINNING she imagined that if she kept going out a bit longer with Kamil, she'd end up seeing Driss again. It wasn't the case. Kamil always wanted to see her alone, the imbecile. He'd say, 'We could go for a spin in my car, if you like.' Or, 'Shall we go up for a smoke on the roof?' They'd drive at full speed on the road to Azemmour, or fall asleep in the sun high above Casa, among the laundry and the giant satellite dishes. They'd wake up to the song of the muezzin summoning the faithful for evening prayer, and all the white roofs would already be orange from the setting sun. It wasn't so bad, to be honest, but if it went on like this, she was never going to see Driss again.

The problem was she couldn't get Kamil to understand she wanted to see people; you can only ask that kind of boy things at the right moment, or he'll panic. Sarah knew how it worked. At the beginning you've got to ask for very simple things.

For example, you say you want to eat sardines, even if the truth is you don't really feel like eating sardines. Making demands like that lets them know you're not just any girl, and anyway sardines are easy enough to find. What happens next is the boy takes you to eat sardines and that makes him feel very pleased with himself. And when a boy is pleased with himself, he's completely overawed by it, starts mixing everything up and thinks that's what love is. Anyway, it's not very complicated. It's only after a while that you can move on to the next stage of demands, like 'I want this bottle of perfume', or 'I want to see lots of people.' At this point she knew it was better not to hurry Kamil, to leave him in peace so he'd pay for sardines and Coca Cola, and kiss him from time to time in exchange. She had another strategy for seeing Driss again—she went to talk to Yaya.

Yaya knew everyone, and no one knew how old he was. No one really knew what he did either, except that he was always hanging around near school, or at the pool café, at the table in the back, eating cans of tuna in oil. He said he had tuna oil running through his veins, and he had to eat cans and cans of it to stay alive. But that was probably a load of rubbish.

One afternoon she pushed open the door of the pool café; there he was, as usual, sitting in the back, eating tuna. She went and sat down opposite him.

'Hi. I'm Sarah.'

He pretended not to see her, but she knew he'd look at her eventually. All the boys looked at her eventually, and Yaya, even if people tended to forget it, was still a boy.

'I've got something to ask you.'

'No.'

He said it like that, without even lifting his eyes from his can of tuna, his mouth glistening with oil. The whole place reeked of his tuna fish, and of cigarettes, weed and the eau de cologne the older boys at school sprayed themselves with.

'Why not?'

'You have nothing, little French girl. You have nothing to give me.'

The way he threw the truth in her face like that upset her. But the self-assurance in Yaya's voice banished the temptation to lie.

'How do you know I have nothing?'

'I know everything.'

He raised his head as he answered and looked at her with such intensity that she thought maybe he did really know everything about her, the grimy mosaic over the washbasin at home, the floor tiles, her mother, every panini she'd ever earned, even what was flowing in her veins—maybe it was true, the thing about tuna oil. He must have seen she was upset, either that or he'd been seduced, because immediately after he let out a sigh and said, 'Okay, what is it you want?'

'Driss.'

He spat out some oil when she said that—through his nose.

'Driss? The rich guy with the motorbike?'

'Yes.'

'A face like yours, and it's Driss you want?'

'Yes.'

He said nothing for several seconds. He wiped his mouth on his sleeve, then used his index finger to pick up one by one all the tiny shreds of tuna he'd just spat out and put them back in his mouth. Then he let out another sigh, and said, 'You must really be shit poor, petite.'

5

Y AYA WAS OFTEN at the pool café, and equally often on the pavement on Rue Al Kabir, near the French lycée, squatting between the traffic light and the Jus Ziraoui snack bar, elbows on his knees, smoking and humming old Tunisian tunes. He told people his mother was Tunisian, and this was the song she used to sing to him there, back when he was young and happy. He said he was going to go back one day, soon, next year for sure—because Sidi Bou Saïd was way better than this lousy pavement, way better than the pool café, the cars, the pollution; he said he'd find his spot in Sidi Bou Saïd, somewhere among the orange and lemon trees that lined the streets, the guitars, the castanets, the white robes, the girls. He'd been saying it for ever, but he still hadn't gone back. Other times Yaya denied it, all the stories about Tunisia, and swore on the tomb of the Prophet that he wasn't singing tunes from Sidi Bou Saïd but *sura* from the Qur'an; that he'd learnt them from his grandfather who'd been to Mecca, and that one day he was going to give up all this bullshit and go to Mecca too. He told other people that his father was

Tunisian, a wealthy shopkeeper from Hammamet. Once he told Chirine his mother had been an actress in Constantine. Anyway. It was complicated.

He often disappeared just before Ramadan. It took a little while for people to notice that Yaya's usual hangouts were vacant—no one on the pavement, no smears of oil on the table. People said he must be around somewhere—a bit like the way the moon is still there even when you can't see it. It was reassuring. Then gradually people would begin to ask, 'Have you seen Yaya lately?' After two or three weeks everyone would decide he must have gone back to Tunisia, like he'd always said he would. After all, surely you can see the moon in Tunisia too. He always turned up eventually, and when anyone asked where he'd been, he'd say, 'But I never left.'

Sarah was expecting him to pull the same trick on her—promise her Driss and then simply vanish. But the day after they spoke at the pool café he turned up for their rendezvous at Jus Ziraoui. Sarah saw him from a distance, squatting and humming something beneath his red baseball cap—probably some Qur'anic *sura* from Sidi Bou Saïd. She was about to sit down beside him, but he scrambled to his feet.

'What are you doing?'

'Sitting down.'

Yaya shook his head in distress.

'You think you can just sit down on my pavement like that?'

He put his skinny arm around Sarah's shoulder and led her into the snack bar.

She'd been there a few times with Kamil, though he loathed the place. He said the milkshakes there were the most revolting in the whole of Casablanca, and if that was what she wanted he could ask the maid to make her one, it would be much nicer. But every time, Sarah stood at the counter jiggling with anticipation, gawping at all the fruit, the bars of chocolate, the milk cartons and the dripping blender. Kamil paid five dirhams and the madness began. She pointed at the fruit, scanning the names: orange! banana! dates! avocado! She asked for chunks of Merendina cake, Henry's biscuits, whole milk, honey. The guy behind the counter cracked jokes as he blended it all up, squashing the occasional cockroach with his elbow. Drink in hand, Sarah headed to the table by the wall, Kamil feeling so nauseous that he kept his arms crossed to avoid touching anything while she drank. She slurped it through a straw with her elbows on the table, the thick mixture rising slowly. Kamil asked her, 'Don't the ants on the glass bother you?' They did not bother her. When she was finished she felt sick, but she always asked for another.

'What do you want?' asked Yaya.

'Nothing.'

She stared at the bananas, the little sablé biscuits, watermelons, crème fraîche, and in her head she could picture all the different combinations.

'Nothing? Are you sure?'

'Yeah.'

Yaya shrugged and asked for orange-strawberry-banana-honey-lemon-cinnamon. He kept his eyes on her while it was being made.

'I'll get it for you, if you like.'

A few minutes later they were sitting on stools by the wall drinking their milkshakes. It was the first time she'd asked for Tofita sweets in hers, and they crunched between her teeth.

'Okay. I'll take you with me whenever I'm delivering to his crew. But after that, it's up to you.'

'All right,' said Sarah, tipping her head back to get the last drops.

Yaya looked at her, amused.

'What are you after from Driss? Rides on his bike?'

Sarah put down her glass.

'I couldn't care less about his bike.'

'Jewellery? Not his style.'

'I don't want jewellery.'

She used the empty glass to squash an ant crossing the table.

'So what do you want?'

Sarah peered at the dead bug through the bottom of the glass; it was a tiny little smudge, she could barely see it through the smeary remains of the fruit. Only the murderer would know there had ever been a crime. It made her laugh.

Her eyes still on the victim, she said, 'I want to marry him.'

They agreed to meet for the first time that same evening. They were going over to Badr's for a pool party.

6

THEY STOOD WAITING outside the large, Moorish, cedarwood front door that was no longer really in vogue. You didn't see riad-style doors or zellige-tiled fountains much anymore in Anfa Supérieur. Now it was all wrought iron gates, plate glass windows, white villas like in Los Angeles and dogs. A minute earlier, as they'd turned into Rue Ibnou Jabir, the labrador belonging to the villa on the corner had barked as they went by. Yaya leapt in fright, then muttered, 'Dirty beast. Who keeps a fucking street dog in their house? They really fancy they're French.' The heavy double doors drew slowly open and a maid appeared, wiping her hands on her apron.

'Welcome, Lalla, welcome, Sidi.' She bobbed her head, smiling. She led them along a little stone path set into the grass. As they made their way among the palm trees and red hibiscus, Sarah counted her footsteps—one, two, three, ten steps, fifteen steps, as many as her street in Hay Mohammadi, and they hadn't even reached the garden yet.

At the end of the path was the pool. It was dark now, and the lit-up pool glowed blue like the spring sky at eight o'clock in the evening in the month of Ramadan, when the sun's just gone down, the stars aren't out yet and everyone's at home breaking the fast around a table laid for iftar. Every evening during Ramadan, every year, she ran from the bidonville to the Corniche, then walked along the Corniche to the Sun. The Sun was a beach club you had to pay to enter, and every time she tried to get in during the day the bouncer threw a shoe in her face. But during iftar, when there was no one else around, she'd jump the barrier and hurry past the restaurant down some dirt steps to the deckchairs on the sand. They were stacked one on top of another. She took off her sandals and clambered up. When she got to the top, she sat down cross-legged and looked out to sea. Then she stretched out, a queen, looking up at the royal blue sky that existed only for her. When it got dark, she sat back up. She jumped back down onto the sand, grazing her knee, spraining her ankle, and went home to Hay Mohammadi.

'*Ahlan*, friends!'

While Yaya was greeting everyone, all Sarah wanted to do was dive into the sky-blue pool—except that there, sitting on a lounger next to Badr playing the guitar, was Driss. Then she remembered that one day she too would have her blue sky all year round, with no barrier to climb over, a pool in her very own kingdom. She sat down on a deckchair next to Yaya.

'Hey, man,' said Badr, his fingers sliding over the guitar strings, 'you're bringing us girls now, are you?' Alain, beside him, laughed. He was drinking whisky and Coke in great gulps, and stroking Chirine's smooth, glossy hair with his free hand. Chirine, her head in his lap, was yawning. Driss had his back to the others—he was playing patience.

'Don't worry, my friend,' said Yaya, taking off his cap. He took out a little plastic-wrapped bundle and put it on the table. 'I've not forgotten you.'

'Serve yourself a drink,' said Badr, getting to his feet.

Alain was already sniffing the weed, practically crushing Chirine's face. 'Stop it,' she said, sitting up, her cry as shrill as the gulls that swoop over the port of Essaouira. As she brushed her hair out of her face, she caught Sarah's eye and smiled. But Sarah didn't care about her. She was only interested in Driss's bent back that was almost vibrating as he obsessively shuffled the cards, as if Badr's guitar, Chirine's squeals, Yaya's weed and she were at the very edge of his world, far away, towards the south, muffled by the dunes of Dakhla. And then Badr came back with the money. Yaya put his arm round Sarah's shoulder:

'I'm off. Can I leave this little princess with you?'

Badr froze. Chirine, open-mouthed, glanced over at Alain who, joint between his fingers, looked taken aback. Driss, noticing the sudden silence, turned his head towards them. His eyes met Sarah's, perhaps he recognized them—instantly, he lowered his gaze.

'Come on, brothers,' said Yaya, 'she's just a little Frenchie, sweet sixteen with no plans for this evening.'

'Sixteen!' said Chirine sharply. 'Your parents let you out like that?'

Sarah shrugged her shoulders and let out a little laugh. 'Yup,' she said. Badr, fixing his huge, dark pupils on her, asked her what her name was, if she was at the French lycée—the same school he'd gone to a few years earlier, like all the rich Moroccans of Casa. 'Yup,' she said again. She used her eyes to convey all the charm she was capable of, all the sincerity and mystery and beauty, everything that her whole life had enabled her to procure what the world gave freely to others: paninis, milkshakes, cinema tickets, bottles of perfume. It worked, as it always did.

All night long they smoked, danced on the lawn, pushed each other into the pool; Sarah had a great time. Driss was still playing cards, but Badr couldn't keep his eyes off her. It was like they were sewn on to her smooth, plump cheeks, and after Yaya had left she said it, like that, insolently:

'Badr, your eyes, it's like they're sewn on to me!' The words came to her just like that. She'd spent the earlier part of the evening altering a dress that her mother had picked up at the Institut Français—a long blue beach robe that might have belonged, at best, to an actress who'd performed at their theatre, or a singer, or the wife of the president of the Cercle Amical des Français, or of the tennis coach from Mohammédia, maybe even a student who'd got rid of a bunch of old clothes before leaving Casa; anyone, basically—Sarah prayed as she sewed—as long as none of these women had ever been seen wearing it by anyone from the lycée. Everything she picked up second-hand she took apart and refashioned until all the curves of the previous owner, all the wrinkles in the fabric made by her movements, the smell, dissolved and died, slain by her scissors.

Badr smiled. 'Well, well. She's not shy, Yaya's little princess.'

He sat down next to her, posing with his guitar, his wet hair smelling of chlorine; he began singing in English, and sometimes instead of a chorus he chanted obscenities in Arabic to the same melody. Everyone laughed. He kept his eyes on Sarah, like two squashed cockroaches attached to her cheeks with big stitches, oozing fat and sweat, repeating the same obscenities even louder, answered by more laughter, though not as hearty as before. He was already a little bit in love with her.

Later, lounging by the sky-blue pool beneath a tall palm tree, Badr and she were blowing smoke rings with Yaya's weed, when he asked the question: 'So who are you?'

Up until then he'd held her hand, spun her round on the grass, splashed her, asked her, 'What does she want to drink, Yaya's little princess?' But he hadn't asked her that. Sarah knew that a boy who's in love doesn't want to know that sort of thing; he wants to love wholeheartedly like you'd love a flower, love like that can last for months, as long as you can't see the roots, the underside of the skin, the dust. But lying there by the pool, neither she nor Badr had been able to think of anything to say to each other for at least ten minutes as they smoked their joint, and a few feet away Alain was bleating like a goat, mimicking the peddler who sold eggs and bleach in the streets of Casa, and Chirine was howling with laughter. Sarah even heard Driss chuckle. So poor Badr had to say something. He couldn't leave them both alone in their silence like that.

'What do you mean, who am I?' said Sarah, as she gazed up at the sheltering palm fronds.

'A beautiful girl like you, sixteen years old, hanging around with dealers and old folk like us, I've never seen anything like it.'

Before she answered, Sarah turned her head to look at him. She still had to unleash all the enchantment of her beauty to distract Badr from the little rundown house in Hay Mohammadi.

'You know who I am.'

'I do?'

He'd also turned his head and was staring at her apprehensively, like a child.

'I'm Yaya's little princess.'

At these words, Badr burst out laughing and Sarah understood it was a laugh of relief.

They stood up and went back to join the others on the sunloungers. Badr was whispering bits of gossip to Sarah, and whenever he got too close she drew back, knowing that this slight recoiling would give birth to all his hopes of seeing her again mingled with doubts and fears, and that these hopes and these doubts and fears would hallow her status as a guest at all Badr's future pool parties until the end of time, or at least until her beauty faded. Even the pool parties that would happen after she married Driss—she'd wear a new blue dress made by someone other than her—she'd still be invited, now she knew it, she'd stroke the water in Badr's pool with the tips of her soft bride's feet, no blisters or grimy toenails, and Badr would watch her, wondering whether he'd have had to have had a bigger pool for her to fall in love him. Yes, he would.

'Chirine, poor girl,' he said to her. 'Half Arab, half Jewish. No one's ever going to want to marry her.'

'What about Alain?'

They looked over at Chirine, who had her arms draped over Alain's shoulders and was kissing his neck.

'Alain's Jewish, he's twenty-four, and there's no one left in Casa. But the minute a proper Jewish girl rocks up, I bet you anything you like, he'll be off.'

Driss kept his distance most of the night, playing cards on his lounger until four in the morning. He blushed when anyone spoke to him and quivered with excitement whenever he heard the word motorbike. He'd say, 'What bike? What make?' Then as soon as the subject changed, he'd go back to his reveries. Chirine, seeing Sarah watch him as she swam, fully clothed, in the pool, murmured, 'Poor guy, it would be so great if he met a girl one day.'

7

SHE WAS WOKEN at six in the morning by *Fajr*, the first prayer of the day. She could feel the rough grain of the sunlounger under her cheek as she turned her head to avoid the light. It made her laugh to be woken up by the mosque and the sun even in a garden in Anfa Supérieur, just like in Hay Mohammadi. Someone had spread a blanket over her and, as she opened her eyes, she saw Chirine moving around, muttering, 'Poor bastard,' fumbling beneath the deckchairs, in the grass, inside a bag. On a nearby lounger, Alain sighed. 'Calm down,' he said. 'Wait a bit, we'll find them later.'

'I can't, it's the third time I've done this to him.' She saw Sarah open her eyes and flung herself towards her. 'Can you see my keys?' Her eyes level with Chirine's knees, Sarah patted the grass and finally felt the keyring clink in her fingers. 'Here they are,' she said. Chirine grabbed the keys and ran down the stone path that led to the gate.

'Her driver's been waiting for her outside the gate all night,' Alain said, propping himself up on his elbow. 'She forgot all about him.' He lay back down and said that Chirine should just buy her driver's licence like everyone else, it wasn't that scary driving around Casa. Alain was small and thin, with the dark skin of a Moroccan Jew, darker than an Arab. He smelt of tobacco and soap. On their way there the previous evening Yaya had told Sarah that Alain was in way over his head, he was still dealing to him for now, but if he carried on like this he was going to stop, and to hell with the money.

'You'll see how thin he is. Weed's not enough for him anymore, he's starting to do heavy stuff.'

'Like what?' asked Sarah.

'Karkoubi, like the street kids. He asks me for it three times a week.'

Abdellah had often offered Sarah karkoubi but she'd never touched it. It was the drug of crazies and criminals, so when she saw Alain last night in the garden for the first time, lit up by the moon, so fragile-looking, singing along, with Badr on guitar, in his wavering voice, she thought Yaya must have got it wrong. But in the morning light she saw the scabs on his skin, in the fold of his elbow, on his neck, the backs of his hands, beneath his shoulder blades. Some were still oozing blood. She could see his teeth were black; one of his top teeth, next to the right canine, had fallen out. And in the sunlight she saw his eyes—ravenous eyes. Sarah knew these ravenous eyes; even when the kids from the bidonville were in the middle of eating they had those eyes, eyes filled with fear that this might be the last time.

'Where do you live?' He'd lain back down on the sunlounger and was smoking kif in a long wooden pipe.

'Right near here,' Sarah lied.

'I'm in Gauthier, but I'll drop you off if you like,' he said, handing her the pipe.

Sarah inhaled deeply. She preferred kif to hash because it was sweet; as she breathed it in, she pressed her tongue against her palate in little taps and swallowed; each drop of saliva was a drop of coconut milk, honey, fermented milk and Pom's soda blended up at Jus Ziraoui.

'That's nice of you, but I'll walk,' she said as she exhaled.

Alain smiled; even with his black teeth, even with the gaping hole behind his canine like one of the tar pools on the Aïn Sebaa road, he had a beautiful smile. It was huge on his bony jaw, and the fine lines, dimples, blemishes and folds of skin surrounded it like a crown made of bronze and chunks of dates.

'You French girls really have no idea,' he said, taking back the pipe.

That was a real rich bastard line. As far as they were concerned, the street was only for dogs and poor people. Poor people were a terrible risk for girls from good families, whose purity would not survive mixing with other social classes; so whenever a rich person, for some absurd reason, had to leave his villa and set foot on the asphalt, it was always, of course, a man. But Alain had to have seen the occasional girl from a good family in the street. Sitting in his driver's old Peugeot 106, he must have caught sight in the rear-view mirror, just above the dangling deodorizing tree, of a young girl in jeans carrying a handbag, no hijab, strolling nonchalantly through the surrounding poverty. And he must have shaken his head, the wooden beads of the seat cover rolling against his back, and muttered, 'Those French girls really have no idea.' A girl in jeans walking down the road could only be a French girl who hadn't grasped the rules.

They were the same French girls who took the bus with the proles, without blinking, instead of taking a taxi or having a driver like the Moroccans from Anfa Supérieur; the ones who bought bread and La Vache Qui Rit for five dirhams from the disgusting *mahlaba* in the Bordeaux quarter instead of lunch at Café Campus. Even if the big money was always the Moroccans, the French in Casa, with their expat contracts and their company rentals, could at least make an effort to spread their money around a bit, Sarah thought. Maybe they didn't understand that money, round here, was the only power that counted, maybe they hoped to make the most of their time in Morocco to—the words revolted her—'put aside some cash'; but it didn't work like that, there was one law for the rich and one for the poor in this country. Kamil always said it was only the French who flouted the very clear social hierarchies to that extent. Sarah agreed. If she had their money, she'd have lunch every day at Café Campus, pizza with black olives, a cheese panini, Coca-Cola, a baghrir pancake with honey and jam. She'd gobble it all up at once, mouth open, chewing the stretchy cheese and syrupy strawberries, licking her fingers—she'd never set foot in a *mahlaba* again, with the poor people and the Séverines of this world. Séverine went to the *mahlaba* every day, as if every lunchtime her big house in the Oasis neighbourhood simply evaporated. She'd started coming out with disgusting things like, 'It's only five dirhams, you'd be a fool not to.' Sarah would see her go into the shop, barely wider than a corridor, and saunter up to the chill cabinet piled high with drinking yoghurts, packets of plain biscuits, cheese and cans of tuna. At the back of the shop there were piles of oranges and Moustache sitting on his stool looking out for flies, his fluorescent pink flyswatter hanging on the wall behind him. He didn't seem to notice the pervasive stink of cheese—the chill cabinet had long since stopped chilling. It was the flies that drove him crazy. He had to kill them all, one by one. In the middle of serving someone, in the middle of pouring a glass of milk or cutting a piece of Edam cheese—everyone called it red cheese, because of the colour of its paraffin wax shell—he'd detect a faint buzzing and freeze. He'd start shooting suspicious looks in all directions to locate the fly—and as soon as he found it, his eyes would open wide; he looked like an owl. The moment of truth. If anyone in the *mahlaba* made the slightest noise, Moustache waved at them to be quiet. Without taking his eyes off the enemy, he slowly picked up the flyswatter behind him and, after a brief pause while he determined his strategy, smacked the wall with all the agility his fat body could muster. Often he got it first go; just as often he missed his mark. When that happened, overwhelmed with a silent, uncontrollable rage, he began beating the air wildly in all directions. It looked almost like he was dancing. Meanwhile more and more people were waiting to be served. You could queue half an hour sometimes at Moustache's *mahlaba*, and if ever someone asked if he was planning to get the chill cabinet repaired, he'd give them a filthy look, as if repairing it would be the most pathetic surrender.

Once the fly had been killed, Séverine, wearing the flared jeans she'd brought back from Paris, took her turn to peer into the chill cabinet and pointed to some yellowing bread rolls that looked like potatoes. Asking for two, she said, '*Jouj, 'afak*,' with her Rif accent—just like her Loubna. If she'd been smart, instead of copying her maid's accent she'd have worked on getting a Fez accent, like all the high-class people in Casa. Sarah tried sometimes but she couldn't quite manage it—she'd learnt all her Arabic from Abdellah, and that idiot really talked like a yokel. She consoled herself with the thought that it was better not to know any Arabic anyway, and only speak French.

With the only fork he had, Moustache would crush the tuna in tomato sauce onto the two rolls Séverine had asked for. One day when his battle against the flies was going well, he had stopped, raised his arms, said, 'Catch, Lalla Sivrine!' and tossed the sandwiches in her direction. Séverine, who'd missed them by a mile, burst out laughing and, while he licked smears of tuna off his fingers, picked them up from the floor. The fact that he called her Lalla, when she shopped every

43

day in his *mahlaba* that stank of cheese and greedily bit into bread that had fallen on the filthy floor, was really the final indignity. But they've got the eye, these old shopkeepers. They can always spot their superiors. Moustache never said to Sarah, 'Catch, Lalla Sarah!'

While Séverine shamelessly ate her sandwiches in front of everyone in the lycée playground, Sarah skulked in the pool café down the road, where the local Yayas and kif smokers hung out all day and sometimes late into the night. They did nothing but loll in the metal chairs, staring into space, flinging insults at each other, and ordering twelve-egg omelettes from Haroun, who ran the place. Haroun lolled around with them and hated getting up. You could wait an hour for a mint tea, and half the time customers went into the kitchen to make their own, leaving a couple of coins on the table as payment. 'Make your own omelette, scumbag,' Haroun would say every time. But then, acquiescing in the face of outraged grunts, threats of bankruptcy, accusations of treachery and general scorn at his laziness, eventually he'd get up from his chair, go into the kitchen, complain there were no eggs and drag himself over to Moustache's shop to buy some.

Sarah went straight upstairs to the first floor, where there were a couple of tables by a large window that looked onto the street. From there, as she first licked the tomato sauce from the tuna then chewed each bite as slowly as if it were gum, she watched the queens, the rich Moroccan girls from the French lycée, with their low-rise jeans and leather handbags, heading for Café Campus, where they would eat for fifty dirhams, using the money their fathers handed them every morning before they climbed into their driver's Renault. They skipped jauntily along the pavement, freezing for a millisecond whenever a street kid brushed too close. It was hard to believe Sarah and they were made of the same flesh. At school, if one of these girls ever looked at her, it was with a gentle, almost apologetic disdain.

But Alain, on his lounger, with his pipe in his mouth, had looked at her with a curious amusement, as if he'd discovered a new little animal whose existence he'd never suspected. The good thing about these older guys who were twenty-four and not yet married was they only hung out with other older people who were twenty-four and not yet married, and there weren't enough of them that they could afford only to hang out with people who were as rich as them. There was a whole world between Badr's house in Anfa Supérieur and Alain's apartment in Gauthier; it was unlikely they'd ever addressed a word to each other back when they were in the same class at the lycée. But when you were twenty-four and you lived in Casa, if you hadn't been smart enough to get out or have kids, you ended up hanging out with whoever you could. So Badr, Alain, Chirine and Driss found themselves together— probably not by choice—driving around the city streets in their big cars like idiots, waiting for something to happen and trying the new drugs that Yaya claimed he'd got from France.

'This is the bomb,' Yaya would say, drawing sachets of cocaine from his pocket. 'Everyone's going mad for it in Paris.'

So even if Sarah didn't have a Rolex, it wasn't like these four were going to put much effort into investigating her. And anyway, it must have been quite nice to have a pretty new plaything, blue and docile, slip into their group without them even asking.

8

It took her a ridiculous amount of time to get back from Anfa Supérieur. She walked down streets lined with palm trees and villas, deserted in the early morning light since the housewives were still asleep and the Jaguars all parked inside. All the streets looked alike, and most of them didn't even have a sign. When Sarah was going to meet someone, they'd say, 'Keep going after the Hotel Suisse, it's the third turning on the right, the second house with a black front door.' Every single time Sarah got lost. She walked back to the street's security guard who was sitting on a stool in his green cabin, head tipped back, snoring. There was a biro and a large spiral-bound notebook on his lap covered in scrawls—the security guards in Casa were officially employed to protect the neighbourhood from thieves, but in reality they noted down the comings and goings of everyone in their sector and reported them to the police. Sarah was about to tap on the window to ask the way when she heard the cry—of all the cries in the world, it was her favourite.

'*Lbiiie!*'

It might have come from three streets away, but she could hear the cry of the *viouzabi* as if he were shouting in her ear, louder than that of the muezzin. And all the beautiful ladies in the villas still lying in bed must have heard him too, shouting in their fine, white, diamond-encrusted ears, and muttered, 'Oh that damned *viouzabi* is at it again,' while downstairs the maids were scurrying—they absolutely mustn't miss the *viouzabi*. The volume of his cry, curiously always at the same pitch from the moment the cart began coming up Anfa Hill, deceived even the sharpest of ears; almost always, by the time the maids had run panting out of the front door he'd already have turned down the next street. They'd have to wait for the next time—it might be the next day or the next week; and meanwhile at teatime their mistresses would complain in their grating voices, 'That stupid maid missed the *viouzabi*, now we're stuck with all this old tat.'

Sarah knew the *viouzabi* too, but from the other side. He'd spend the morning in his cart going round the wealthy neigh-bourhoods, picking up all the stuff that the Chirines and Badrs of this world didn't want anymore—crockery, soft toys, chairs, old clothes—'vieux habits', which is how he got his name. Then he went and sold them to poor people in the centre of the city for almost nothing. Sarah and her mother had bought loads of things from him, but their best buy had been an electric fan for eight dirhams that had only one broken blade. She knew his old, brown face that shone like wax slashed with a knife, and his small eyes, and his crocheted *sheshia* like an Algerian imam's hat. Sarah knew that the day she moved into Anfa she would blank him, avoid his gaze while she tossed her silk scarves into the cart—maybe she'd wear sunglasses—but even with the best will in Morocco and the world, she'd never be able to not recognize him. Happily, he was highly unlikely to recognize her—he was a businessman, after all.

Even so, she ran towards the sound of his voice now, full of bounce after her night on a sunlounger, and perhaps from the kif too. She took a wrong turning several times before she located the cart parked by a hedge, gradually filling up with the pile of plates and bowls that a gardener was carefully cradling in his arms. When she drew near, the *viouzabi* said, 'You, girl, you're not from here.' He wasn't fooled by her dress. Poor people look each other in the eye.

It was the *viouzabi* who took her home. She did the rounds of all the wealthy neighbourhoods with him until ten a.m., perched on the side rail like a duchess in a horse-drawn carriage, waving graciously at the dogs, or calling out with him. Then he began to complain, 'You're too heavy, kid,' so she got down. Within two minutes she was bored. She began doing sidesteps, hops, pirouettes. She said, 'Aren't you hot, *viouzabi*?' and the old man laughed. He had more money than her, for sure, with his wily business sense; but she at least could still pretend. When you start doing a poor person's job everything changes, you get dirty looks when you go into shops. It's all over then. It was honestly better not to work if you wanted to maintain a shred of dignity.

When she got home, she found her mother asleep on the sofa. She was snoring louder than the guard in Anfa, with an irregular rumble that from time to time blew out snot from the back of her nose. She could have been a security guard if the little green cabins had been big enough to contain her hundred and ten kilos—and if she'd ever wanted to work. Her ankles were violet and swollen, like her calves, her toenails were black, and she had a goitre that shuddered in time with the sound coming from her throat, a white goitre with a red patch of eczema, but mostly white—not like Sarah whose skin was the colour of terracotta. 'You look like your father, he was dark like you are,' Monique told her. 'Your father the soldier,' she'd say, 'the soldier, as handsome as Marlon Brando.' Other days she said he was a rich shopkeeper, a stage actor or an opera singer. Whatever; he'd done a bunch of different things. The only father Sarah had ever really known was Fat Joe, even if he never said much. They'd lived in his apartment for years and years back in Cannes. Her mother went to the market, and he paid for school. Everything was fine, but when Sarah was ten, Fat Joe began getting this creepy expression on his face whenever he looked at her, so Monique had taken her and a suitcase and they'd gone to sleep at crazy Rita's, the clairvoyant. They slept on the sofa, which was big enough for them both, because Sarah was little, and her mother wasn't fat yet. Then there was Didier, who had a moustache and told them about Morocco, that it was better there, the three of them could open a shop. They packed their bags and said goodbye to Rita, who foresaw a marvellous future for them with many pieces of gold. Once they got to Casa, Didier took all their money and cleared off, and lo and behold there was never any shop. And here they were.

'Maman,' Sarah said, shaking her shoulder. She had nothing to say to her—they generally didn't have much to say to each other—but the sofa was where Sarah slept, and she was tired. Monique was always there, dribbling all over everything that wasn't hers, even though she had her own room. Sarah never took her bed, because she was respectful, and because it made her feel nauseous to have the dirty sheets where some old guy from the Cercle Amical des Français or the Games Society had slept touching her terracotta skin. They never stayed the night. When one or other came over too often, Sarah would whine, just for form's sake, and get upset, and Monique would say, 'Be quiet, dammit, it's thanks to him we eat.'

'Maman!'

Monique rubbed her eyes.

'What time is it?'

'Eleven,' said Sarah.

Lowing like a cow, Monique hoisted all her kilos one by one until she was sitting up. At the end of the operation she passed her hands over her face and through what was left of her hair.

'What have you been up to, getting home at this hour, I swear.'

And she got to her feet. Whenever Sarah came home late, Monique would come out with these exact words, and then she'd stand up. The truth was, she didn't care what Sarah had been up to, so she added 'I swear' to make it clear it wasn't a question. It was one of those maternal phrases she came out with, as if she were performing a role. There were others, like, 'Don't get into drugs,' when Sarah sat in front of the house smoking kif, or, 'Work hard at school.' They both thought it sounded right, sounded normal, like an English pop song. It didn't matter if other words came out later in the evening, when the dark sky drew the curtain on their pretence.

Sitting cross-legged on her sofa in some orange pyjamas she'd bought from the *viouzabi*, Sarah was eating a fourth Merendina. She had chocolate smeared around her mouth and empty wrappers in her lap. Monique watched her pensively in the light of the bare bulb; just before she got up to go and meet one of her wrinkly old boyfriends from the Cercle, she murmured, as though to herself, 'You and your pretty face, you won't have to do a day's work in your life.'

9

THE NEXT TIME was at La Notte. Yaya came by to pick her up in his taxi—sometimes he drove a taxi. 'It belongs to a brother, we go *ness-ness*,' which meant going halves, and also meant milky coffee. Ever since Sarah had realized that boys were ready to pay for endless coffees to get her to sit opposite them at a table at Café Campus so they could look at her, she took to ordering one *ness-ness* after another, gulping it down and then immediately gesturing to the waiter and demanding 'another *ness-ness*!' To say it properly you had to pronounce just the consonants, it required a certain fierceness, a brisk jerk of the head, like a crouching leopard ready to pounce, a leopard who suddenly stuck out a serpentine tongue forked at the tip and attacked, hissing, *'ness-ness.'* She repeated the game frenetically, inexhaustible. The boy sitting opposite watched as she drained her cup then raised an arm, tapping the dirty table with impatient fingers, irritated, until at last another *ness-ness* arrived and with it the instant reprise of the little spectacle. Once she began to feel like she might vomit, she asked for some Sidi Ali and the conversation could begin.

'Are you going to make me pay for the ride?' She was standing in front of her house in a gold lamé dress she'd nicked from a stall at the Maarif market. It was midnight. Yaya, in the red taxi, nonchalantly took off his fake Ray-Bans.

'Come on, get in.'

When it was Yaya's turn to have the taxi, he'd drive round Casa for weeks on end, tooting the horn like a nutter, playing a cassette of the music from his cousin's wedding on a loop, singing and clapping to the rhythm of the *darboukas* instead of keeping his hands on the wheel. He probably never even picked up any clients.

Behind the fence in the bidonville, Abdellah roared with laughter. '*Hayhay*, Lalla Sarah,' he said, 'what's that dress you're wearing, you off to see the king, or what?' Behind him his mother, leaning against the scrap metal wall breastfeeding her youngest daughter, said, 'Shush, Abdellah.' She didn't like any mention of the king, she was afraid of the police.

They sped down the Corniche with the windows down— because there were no windows—and Yaya said, 'It's going to be wild tonight at La Notte.' Then he teased her, 'You'll never get your hands on Driss, he wouldn't look at a pauper like you.' When they got there, Yaya left the taxi in the middle of the road. He walked right up to the head of the queue, one arm around Sarah's shoulder, and shook the bouncer's hand. 'She's with me.'

The gang was in the back with a load of other people— rich girls from the lycée, married couples with fancy watches, middle-aged single guys, a few hookers. La Notte was the only place in Casa where you could still dance rock and roll and slow dances on a Saturday night. They got into pairs to dance to Elvis Presley, lifting their feet, making waves with their hands, the girls twisting and twirling and ending up breathless and giggling, heads upside down, spines curved over a forearm. It was dizzying. But in among all the twirling there was one boy who sat slumped, as if nailed to the red leather banquette, the strange, green-tinted shadow of his crooked nose projected onto the wall behind him. It was Driss, holding a glass of mint cordial. He looked glum. But the moment the chorus rang out, his upper body began to jerk back and forth in time to the music, until he spilt his drink on his jeans. He stopped and glanced around uneasily, as if to make sure he hadn't been seen. Sarah, amused, turned to Yaya, but he'd gone.

Driss was a tricky sort of boy to understand, because he wasn't really like a boy. Sarah knew exactly what made boys tick, from Kamil, Badr and all the little half-wits from last year, to the old guys from her mother's social clubs who weren't so very different except they were ugly. She knew that a boy is someone who never stops staring, worse than the police, casting their eyes all over girls' bodies, approving, disciplining and monitoring, as if they belonged to them. When one fine morning women started hiding their faces behind the hijab, no one in Casa was remotely shocked. Everyone said: Can't blame them, poor things, they're just tired of it all. Driss though, with his sliding eyes, might live in the most beautiful house in Anfa, but he never behaved like anything belonged to him. He barely spoke. Sarah had noticed the way boys jabbered away at her all the time, maybe because she was so quiet; she knew perfectly well they got annoyed with girls who talk, even girls as pretty as her. The chatty ones like Chirine who made their presence felt infuriated them, as if they couldn't bear to see their space stolen from them by a body that was meant to be controlled but that now seemed dangerous, untamed. It frightened them, this wildness. Sarah understood that boys were for the most part very fragile and one had to take great care not to upset them.

She sat down next to Driss on the red banquette, her terracotta knee almost touching his jeans. He was staring into space, drink in hand, a fixed grin on his face. She thought she felt him stiffen. She shifted her leg a little to reveal her thigh, its tiny blond hairs standing on end. She sat and watched the dancing, beautiful, docile, silent, reassuring, perfectly correct. He didn't look at her. He didn't jabber. Driss and Sarah sat frozen alongside each other on a banquette in La Notte, a fixed grin on each of their faces now, their bodies tense among the shadows and the glinting light of the mint cordial, watching all those people of flesh and blood, vivacious, with their explosive laughs, watching the whores enjoying themselves.

The first slow began; on the dancefloor couples who'd been dancing rock and roll pulled apart, there was a general murmuring, a pause; the girls on banquettes sat up straight, legs crossed, hands on their knees. The boys standing around cast their eyes about; many of them landed on her, like twenty torch beams trained on the source of a noise. Sarah knew she had to act quickly. With an airy movement that sent her curls flying about her face, she turned to Driss.

'D'you want to dance?'

He started, almost knocking his drink over. But at last he looked at her. His eyes had never been so close. His irises seemed to be shuddering, and not because of the lights. Sarah would find out soon: it was a tic of fear he often displayed, as if he was constantly unnerved by this changing Morocco.

'No.'

It was the curt kind of *no* that Sarah spat at kerb-crawlers when she was walking around town, guys who called from their cars, 'Hey, gazelle, come for a ride.' She had no time to respond; Badr was approaching. He'd got there before the others, with his big, wobbly belly, his sewn-on eyes filled with courage. He held out his hand, a little breathless: 'Would you like to dance?'

She got up half-heartedly, her eyes vacant. Badr was already tugging her towards the dancefloor when she let go of his hand and went back to Driss. She leant towards him and glared, furiously, the way men glare at women to stop them getting away. And she said to him, 'I'm in love with you.'

Then she turned back to the dancefloor where Badr was waiting for her. As they danced *le slow* she saw that Driss hadn't moved—he was still staring into space, mint cordial in hand, shoulders slumped, a fixed smile on his face. But now his leg was jiggling.

I O

SARAH HAD HEARD declarations of love from her mother's mouth loads of times, when she wanted to get Fat Joe to buy cheese at the market in Cannes. She'd heard them in the bidonville, when Abdellah's sister married a boy who was better than her, who was going to get her out of there—he was the driver for a family in the Californie neighbourhood. Basma had gone off all smiling to live with that bastard somewhere grim in the centre of town, then she came back for Eid covered in bruises. No one said anything. Even prostitutes said *I love you* when they got pregnant and had to make the guy marry them quick so they didn't end up in prison with the other daughter-mothers, their kid in an orphanage. A lot of them got abortions in the backs of restaurants, but half the time they died, haemorrhaging over chairs covered in beach towels; marrying some loser seemed more tolerable. The prostitutes shouted at the tops of their voices at all the men they knew, *I love you, or you, or you.* The truth was, no one wanted anything to do with them. The boys at the lycée, who'd been going to see them since they were thirteen, said they were scum, as though they were lesser women; a woman is supposed to have dignity. Yet Sarah found them very dignified, with their fearless expressions, their own money, their proud breasts and their freedom from husbands. They were untamed—maybe people didn't like prostitutes not because they were lesser women, but because they were too much women.

That was why Sarah always said *I love you* to the boys she went to bed with. It was the only way to forgive herself for being touched by them, the only way to allow herself to carry on accepting their gifts. She had to say it convincingly to be believed, but it was hard. However hard she tried, every time she uttered the words she heard hunger in her voice—the same hunger as in her mother's voice as she stared at the cheese in the market. It was unmistakeable—a person hearing it from miles away would know that the girl who'd said it hadn't had any lunch. They'd hear hope in her intonation as well, the same as Basma's hope that she'd have electricity one day; and they'd pick up the prostitutes' dread of ending up behind bars. Sarah knew perfectly well it was audible, but she couldn't help herself; that was the accent in which she'd learnt to read. In La Notte that night with Driss it was an emergency that necessitated the use of the formulation, but it was the same thing, the same accent—she was genuinely dying of hunger that evening, and burning with hope for a better life, and in immense distress at the idea that he would understand—precisely because of that distress—that she didn't really love him. Really loving someone, she knew what that was, and this wasn't it—she'd experienced that the year before, with Zineb. She'd never forgotten it.

Zineb had rectangular glasses, black frizzy hair, a long, horsy face and she smelt of harissa. At the beginning of their first maths class of the year, Sarah saw her from a distance as she arrived, successively accomplishing each of the things she was most afraid of: walking to her desk, third row, room 86 in Building L, putting down her blue backpack covered in ballpoint doodles, pulling out her chair, saying, 'Can I sit here?' with those victim's eyes—eyes it was impossible to say no to. It wasn't that Sarah didn't like harissa. It was simply that, for obvious reasons, it didn't do to be seen with a girl like Zineb—the kind of girl who got on the school bus to the lycée without batting an eyelid, got off the bus, smiling, at the back entrance of the building, and didn't even bother to walk round to the main entrance so she could pretend she'd been brought to school by her driver like everyone else. French students got their education at the Casablanca lycée for free. The others got it in return for tens of thousands of dirhams and gifts on top—flowers, or VIP membership of the Sun Club, or a stay at the Mamounia in Marrakech, or sometimes even a car, depending on the father's line of work. Apparently plane tickets worked best—in Sarah's class alone there were three boys whose fathers were executives at Royal Air Maroc. Since there were practically no more French people left in Casa, the apartment buildings that had once been the glory of the protectorate now swarmed with the three thousand offspring of Moroccan businessmen, with the last remaining Séverines still hanging on along with a few kids of mixed couples and in among them, dissonant and strange, glimpses of dark skin: the ill-starred skin of girls like Zineb.

They wouldn't have been able to pay for even a week at the lycée if their mothers hadn't had the inspired idea of becoming teachers or nurses there. Everything about them exuded lower middle class—they wore colourful tunics from the market in Hay Hassani, bought schoolbooks second-hand from people they knew in the year above, ate in the school canteen. Sometimes, by accident, Sarah passed them in the playground wearing a new pair of jeans she'd been given by Kamil or some other guy, walking fast and speaking to no one. That was her rule: to speak as little as possible, unless someone spoke to her first, preferably a boy with a nice watch; she might not seem rich, but at least no one could tell quite how poor she was. Walking rapidly and quietly, she surprised a couple of Zinebs talking to each other in Arabic, though they spoke French perfectly. '*Fiyya jouu',*' said one, tapping her tummy—I'm hungry—and the other girl responded unashamedly in Arabic. Sarah hurried past, propelled by the fear of being seen with them, dismayed that someone could know the language of the dominator yet voluntarily choose to speak the language of the poor and the oppressed. She was revolted by such a contented acceptance of poverty—even though Sarah was poorer than them, she at least still had enough pride to keep protesting this reality. Her hurried footsteps, new jeans paid for with her skin, furtive lunches upstairs at the pool café, her taciturnity, were as much a refusal of her situation as they were acts of guerrilla warfare.

Sarah didn't so much as glance at Zineb during the maths lesson—she had to make it clear they weren't from the same world, even though they were from exactly the same world—the world of the maidless and the driverless. Except for the detail that Zineb ate tajine once a month because her mother had resigned herself to teaching Arabic to a class of eleven-year-olds. But Zineb didn't get it at all. Every single maths lesson she came and sat down next to Sarah, cheerful and naïve, every maths lesson she said, 'Bonjour,' with a big smile on her face, as if she didn't see the fundamental difference between them—that of war. When they had an affine transformation to solve in class, and Sarah, crossing her arms and legs, sighed and stared into space, filled with contempt for the teacher who somehow imagined she would stoop to showing an interest in such an exercise, which would never be of any use to her, Zineb would ask with concern, 'You okay? D'you understand what we have to do? D'you want me to explain?' She could solve all the equations. She revised in free periods and during her lunch break. She finished tests ten minutes before the rest of the class. 'I couldn't care less about these exercises,' said Sarah, and there was a fleeting wave of alarm behind Zineb's thick glasses, as if it were not possible to not give a damn about these exercises. And she would launch into a fevered explanation, exhaling with her spicy breath—'You see the variable x, *yak*? You see the constants now?' She went on and on until Sarah couldn't help but vaguely listen. And she'd end up listening when at breaktime Zineb told her you had to work when you were lucky enough to go to a school like this, it was important if you were to have what she called a nice life. She was going to study medicine, she said, at the University of Casablanca, even though it was almost all boys there: she was going to be a paediatrician and save children's lives. And whether Sarah wanted to hear it or not, Zineb told her about the lamb slaughtered in the bathtub for Eid—blood spurting everywhere because her cousin didn't know how to do it properly—or her grandmother's journey to Mecca, where she was hoping to die so she would go straight to paradise. One month later she still hadn't died and she had to come back to Morocco—the hotel was expensive and her husband was calling her every three days from the phone booth opposite the house, complaining it was inhuman to leave him like that, he couldn't cook, he was going to die of hunger before she died if she carried on like this and there was no way she'd be setting foot in paradise guilty of such a crime. Then Zineb told her about her little brother Amine, who refused to get up to eat before sunrise during Ramadan; 'There's no way he's fasting,' she said, 'given he hangs out with all the street kids, the *chemkara*. And they all drink alcohol,' she added, sounding aghast, and when she uttered these forbidden words she murmured an incantation of protection—'*Allah yahafedna.*' When she saw Sarah after school jumping into an older guy's Porsche, she giggled, covering her mouth—she'd never so much as kissed a boy. She told Sarah that as well.

And then one day, towards the end of Ramadan, while she was telling Sarah her mother's recipe for *briouates*, she said, 'What are you doing tonight? Why don't you come over for iftar?'

I I

THIS WAS TRUE LOVE; the kind that until you've grasped its contours, felt its flesh, wanted to die, you can only foolishly utter its empty syllables, maybe attach to it some vague images. Sarah had walked into the apartment block utterly ignorant of it.

To get there, she'd taken the bus with Zineb. The ticket was thirty centimes and the bus stank of sweat right down to the fabric covering the seats. When there was no boy to pay for a taxi home from school, she chose to walk for two hours rather than sit on the bus next to some loser shopkeeper snuffling every three seconds like a pig for ten minutes, then wiping the snot on the arm of his jumper. Sometimes acne-scarred teenagers got on and threw themselves on the maids sitting in the back, touching their breasts before running back up to the front of the bus when the women started to wave their arms around and shout, 'Aren't you ashamed of yourselves, you little shits,' but without getting out of their seats, so as not to get the boys worked up even more. Men laughed and muttered obscenities, while the loser shopkeepers just sat there swallowing their own snot; there were flies, dank scraps of bread on the floor and dried pigeon shit on the windows. Even though Zineb lived in an apartment in the middle of town, and the staircase was lined in shiny grey mosaic and smelt of piss, and she had to walk up six flights because there was no lift, it was better to be holed up there out of sight than to risk being seen on a Casablanca bus that only the truly wretched rode.

'*Marhaba, binti!*'

Welcome, my daughter—it was Chadia, Zineb's mother, who opened the front door. She was short, with a round face, glasses and a pink headscarf. She kissed Sarah on both cheeks and with her hands on her shoulders exclaimed in Arabic, 'Aren't you pretty!' Then with a wide smile she took her arm—'*Yallah*,' she said—and led her down a dark corridor, as though leading a young bride to the marriage ceremony, whispering conspiratorially in her ear, 'You're so pretty, you must be careful, you know? Stay home, behave and you'll find a good husband, *insh'Allah*.' Sarah threw an amused glance at Zineb, who was following behind and giggling. In the living room she felt Chadia's plump arm around her shoulder, as though they were old friends—'This is Zineb's French friend,' she crooned, 'her name is Sarah.' There were three people sitting on a carved wooden bench with large, red, gold-fringed cushions. Zineb's brother Amine, her grandfather who couldn't cook and her grandmother who still wasn't dead were slouched, mouths agape, in front of the television, watching an episode of *Marimar*, the telenovela that played on a loop at the pool café. The volume was so high that at first Sarah didn't hear the grandmother summon her, patting the bench: 'Come and sit down, young lady, come and sit.' She sat down and the old lady grasped her arm and lifted it: 'You are much too thin. You must eat.' On a low table made from a large round copper-coloured tin tray was a dish of couscous, a bottle of full-fat Salim milk and bowls of dates and *chebakia* soaked in honey, but no one had touched a thing.

'We have to wait,' said Zineb's mother. 'But you're not fasting. Help yourself.'

'I'll wait with you,' said Sarah.

She turned her head like everyone else to look at the television, where Marimar was running along a Mexican beach. She had curly hair and dark skin like Sarah. Zineb's grandfather excitedly pointed his finger at Sarah, then at the television, then back at Sarah, making deep, lowing sounds in Amazigh. 'It's true, you do look like her,' said Zineb, and her mother nodded. It must have been an old episode, because Marimar was still shabby and poor and barefoot. At the pool café they were already up to the episode where she'd become rich thanks to Gustavo, her secret billionaire father.

'Brigitte Bardot!'

Sarah flinched and the grandmother fixed her with a look, eyes creased, as though trying to peer beneath her skin. She kept saying, 'Brigitte Bardot, Brigitte Bardot,' banging Sarah hysterically on the back. Chadia said, 'You don't know what you're talking about, Mama, Brigitte Bardot is blonde,' and the old lady sighed with frustration and hunched over a little more where she sat. Marimar was struggling in a man's grasp—he had seen her steal some carrots from a garden and was demanding a kiss in return for his silence. 'Son of a bitch,' said Amine, checking the time on the wall clock; the wealthy heir Sergio was already on his way to save Marimar from the man's claws.

This was love; true love, whose existence she had never even imagined. It had appeared for no reason, giving Sarah no warning of the thunderbolt that was about to vibrate through her whole body, down to her toenails—there it was, in a split second: the second Marimar met Sergio's eyes at last, after the fight. That was when everything changed. Wind swirled slowly in the tangled, sandy hair of the young street girl, and circling her dark eyes was a cello, an organ, all the harps in Mexico, and not a single clock. This was true love, yes. Sarah understood then and for evermore that there is no love without wind, without music, without heroes and without danger, without being on the other side of the ocean; and that everyone around her who claimed to be in love merely thought they were.

A little high-pitched chime rang out. 'It's time,' cried Chadia. Everyone reached for the bowl of dates, but Sarah didn't take her eyes off the television screen as the closing credits rolled, a reel of names like so many boys courting her in their convertibles. Suddenly all her boyfriends seemed minuscule, with weak expressions, and she thought she was pathetic to be satisfied with sham love affairs, not even the tiniest breeze or the faintest sound of a cello. She promised herself she would never accept a milkshake from any of them ever again.

She kept her promise for a whole two weeks, and then she got thirsty.

12

SARAH RANG CHIRINE'S DOORBELL at a quarter past five, as they'd planned the night before at the 17 Storeys bakery after La Notte. 'It's easy, you'll see, it's the only red house in the whole of Anfa,' Chirine had told her. Taking a bite of her mushroom quiche, she'd explained to Sarah that you're not allowed to paint houses red in Casa, but because her mother came from Marrakech she found all the white really depressing, she wasn't used to it. Whenever the police showed up, she'd offer them coffee and the maid would make them *msemens* with honey. The walls were brick red, the same red as the lumps of *aker fassi* that Sarah used to shoplift from Aïcha Parfumerie when she was younger— she'd look at her reflection in the shop window on her way out and lick the tip of her index finger and rub it on the earthenware shell coated in red poppy powder. Her finger would turn red and she'd rub it on her lips, and suddenly she had the mouth of a woman, the colour of blood, of dried flowers, of the ramparts of Marrakech, and, she realized as she stood waiting at the front door, of Chirine's house, one of the nicest in Anfa Supérieur. Sarah heard heavy steps coming to let her in.

'17 Storeys!' Alain had shouted the night before at La Notte. He was standing on a chair, waving his arms about wildly. Sarah was still dancing with Badr; the slow dances were over; they were playing disco again now. She was shaking Badr off with pirouettes, shoulder flings, little steps faster than a tap shuffle, exhausting him so that he wouldn't want to try and kiss her—Badr's cheeks were bright red as he attempted, excruciatingly, to keep up, and he was sweating so much that all the black hairs on his chest showed through his white shirt. At the signal from Alain he said, 'Shall we go?' and mopped his forehead with his sleeve. Sarah turned and saw that Driss was no longer sitting on the banquette. He wasn't outside either. She climbed into Badr's car, glancing out of the window whenever she heard the sound of a motorbike.

It took them five minutes to get to Bourgogne. On the bakery's orange façade the word 'Storeys' was painted in large black letters preceded by the number seventeen in white. It was right across from the tallest building in Casa, seventeen storeys high, so naturally that's what it was called. People queued there until seven in the morning for disintegrating quiches or black olive pizzas that had lost their black olives. Yellowing cheese croissants that no one ever bought sat in the window for weeks. Everyone always ended up there after La Notte, and because it was cheap sometimes there were guys in shabby clothes who'd just tumbled out of Bouss-Bouss, the bar next door. Slowly chewing crumbly pastries, they stared lewdly at the girls at the La Notte table—there were no girls at Bouss-Bouss, because girls like Zineb who lived in the city didn't dare go clubbing, for fear of being called whores. On the pavement outside, beggars held out their hands to people as they went in, imploring, 'Give me, please, give me, please.' A few weeks before, a woman had held on to Sarah's ankle as she was going in with Kamil. 'Lalla, please,' she pleaded. Sarah looked down and saw her sitting cross-legged on the ground, her eyes grey-white, as though her tears had washed away their colour. 'God bless you, Lalla, please, God bless you,' she repeated, speaking fast in a single breath, gripping Sarah's ankle tightly with her swollen blue hands. Sarah froze. Kamil, who had gone ahead without her, turned.

'Sarah?'

She looked up at him. She could still hear the woman on the ground pleading, saying, 'You are so pretty, Lalla.'

'Just give her a kick and she'll let go,' said Kamil. Sarah knew that was what you did; either that or you politely tried to extricate yourself so you wouldn't go to hell, saying 'Amen' after the woman's muttered prayers, promising you'd be back. But she didn't move. She felt sick all of a sudden, a familiar nausea that came to her whenever she caught the eye of one of those people from below, the ones who bowed and scraped when they took her for someone different to them. Sarah never wanted to vomit when it was the rich kids from the lycée who thought she was one of them—but those washed-out eyes

72

had this way of throwing all the colours she'd stolen back in her face. Kamil came back a few minutes later and handed the woman a cheese croissant.

Driss didn't come to 17 Storeys that night after La Notte. Badr brought Sarah the pizza and can of Hawaï she'd asked for, but she took a few seconds to notice—she couldn't take her eyes off the door. Each time it swung open she hoped a squat body with eyes of thyme would materialize, but it always let her down as it swung shut again.

'Aren't you eating?' said Chirine, who was sitting on her left. Alain and Badr were listening to Laïla, daughter of the biggest canned tuna wholesaler in Morocco, as she told them everything Majid had said and done earlier on at La Notte and tried to discern the slightest sign that he was in love— Majid worked in a bank and his parents didn't have a penny, but Laïla was already thirty-four, so she didn't even mind.

'Maybe he's just shy,' said Alain.

Irritated, Laïla said, 'For fuck's sake, I've been trying to get him to understand for a year.'

That was when Sarah turned to Chirine and said, 'I'm in love with Driss.'

She'd suddenly realized she had to hem him in with her love. There was no other solution. Everyone around him had to be told, he had to hear about Sarah from everyone: 'Sarah, do you know Sarah's in love with you?' She had to make it so that he couldn't take a step without feeling the beating of her loving heart beneath his feet, so that the air grew warm, floral-scented, sticky, stifling, so that every face he saw was the face of this one girl. It wouldn't take him a year; under pressure from the entire universe, he'd have to give in.

'Sorry, what did you just say?' Chirine made her repeat her confession twice. 'That's incredible!' she exclaimed—Alain looked over in surprise—then she whispered delightedly, 'I can't believe it, if you knew how long we've been waiting for this, Driss, you know—well I mean you must have guessed, he's not exactly—with girls, I mean—you know what I'm saying—but he's such a great guy, you won't regret it.' Her tone grew serious and solemn; she took a paper serviette and sketched something with an oily finger, as if she were trying to find the way out of an invisible labyrinth—she was trying, she explained, to think of a plan to get Driss and Sarah together without the others. Sarah interrupted every so often with suggestions. 'Shhh!' said Chirine. 'Let me think.' She scratched her head, took another bite of quiche, wiped her mouth, stared into space. Eventually she had an idea.

'One thing Driss never says no to is taking people home. Even if he's running late, or it means going right out of his way, if someone's stuck for how to get home he'll always give them a lift on his motorbike.'

Driss was going over to the red house the following afternoon at five to check out Chirine's father's motorbike, which he was thinking about buying. They decided that Sarah would ring at the door fifteen minutes later, and then leave at the same time as Driss, and he'd give her a lift home on his motorbike.

———

74

As she stood at the red front door, listening for the sound of footsteps, she imagined sitting behind him on the growling motorbike with her arms around his body, pressing her fingers into his podgy stomach. The wind would sting her face and her black hair would fly into those eyes of thyme, making it difficult for him to see the road properly. He'd say, 'Your hair is in my eyes, I can't see the road,' and she'd laugh: 'Who cares about the road!' Maybe those heavy footsteps were his, coming to open the door, or perhaps it was the gardener, or Chirine's father; they'd take her to the garage where she'd find him, entirely focused, checking the back brakes. Sarah heard the latch click; she tugged her sweater and took a deep breath. The door swung open—it was Chirine. Her eyes were red and teary.

'You're late,' she said, sniffing, then turned around and began to cross the garden. She walked quickly, with the occasional hiccupping sob, and Sarah struggled to keep up, looking around at the date palms, bushes and little ponds filled with water lilies glistening among the columns. They went into the entrance hall, which was as empty as the sitting areas beneath the portico.

The walls were plastered in maroon tadelakt that glowed as red, soft and lustrous as the moist interior of a cheek, and the space, though vast, suddenly seemed narrow to Sarah, as though it were shrinking as she walked. She saw floor lamps, large carved wooden tables covered in wares from the Marrakech souk, Berber wool carpets. She almost barged into a maid. It wouldn't have taken much for the tiny woman with her apron half undone to lose her balance as she hurried past Sarah and Chirine. The maid headed for the other end of the room, a bottle in one hand and a wad of cotton wool in the other. It wasn't until she reached one of the sofas that Sarah saw there was a woman in a beige djellaba lying there; she blended in so perfectly with the fabric of the sofa that she'd been completely invisible up until then. The maid tipped the contents of the bottle onto the cotton wool and then wiped the woman's face with it; the woman groaned in pain at her touch.

'Don't worry, it's only my mother,' Chirine said without slowing down.

They went up one flight of stairs and another, then a few steps along a corridor to a bedroom where sunshine lit up the pink sheets, stuffed toys and dressing table of a little girl. Chirine walked across the room and opened two large French doors that led onto a terrace. In a monotone, her eyes lowered, she explained that the terrace looked onto the garage, where Driss was with her father and the motorbike, so Sarah could keep an eye out for him leaving.

'Okay,' said Sarah, trying and failing to catch her eye. 'I'll keep a look out then.'

She leaned over the balustrade. From there she could see the path lined with bushes that led to the brick garage in which were parked in single file the chauffeur's old Citroën, a black Audi and what looked like a Mercedes—it was practically swallowed up inside so she couldn't make out the metal star on top of the bonnet. Alongside it—it looked like an S class—she could just see, protruding from the entrance, the back wheel of a motorbike. Sarah shivered. The engine growled. The tyre vibrated and an orange light blinked on then went off again. A moment later a hand appeared, tenderly caressing the mudguard. Sarah heard the distant mumble of voices; one of them had the high-pitched inflection she had come for.

'There he is,' she said, with a nervous laugh, turning towards Chirine, who didn't reply. She was leaning against the French window inspecting her feet.

'You okay?' Sarah asked. Chirine looked up at her with bloodshot eyes.

'If she doesn't want my father to hit her,' she said, 'why does she get back from the market at four in the afternoon?' She put her head in her hands and began to cry.

Generally, Sarah had no sympathy for people who cried, and the only thing she was interested in just then was Driss, down there, just a few metres away. Her mother wept in front of the *viouzabi* to get him to give her free crockery, and even Sarah had been known to shed a little tear when the police caught her pinching stuff from a market stall—every time, they'd see her damp eyes and say, 'All right, go on, get out of here, we'll forget about it this time.' It was good to cry in front of boys now and then too, for no reason, just to make yourself seem delicate. So she wasn't going to rise to Chirine's bait. But then Chirine spoke.

She said she couldn't stand it anymore at home, she was going to get her own place, she wasn't married, yes, exactly, she wasn't married and she didn't care, she wasn't scared, and if her father didn't want to pay for it, for the apartment, she'd get a job, she'd work every day, he'd be fucking ashamed at her working like that every day and all the old folk would say, 'What a disgrace, Chirine had to get a job, her old man's run out of money,' or something, and he wouldn't be able to look anyone in the eye anymore and it would serve him right.

Watching Chirine sobbing her heart out, Sarah was transported back to when she was a little girl and she still talked to people. One Christmas Day at the Cercle Amical des Français she was playing hopscotch with a blonde girl when a lady with pearl earrings came over to talk to her. 'Which one is your mummy?' she asked with a kind smile, and Sarah naïvely pointed to her mother, sitting by the wall with a plastic cup in her hand, fat and alone. She didn't see the look of disgust in the woman's eyes when she asked her if it was true they lived way out of the city, beyond the railway station, in Hay Mohammadi, by the Carrières Centrales; if it was true that sometimes men came and stayed at their house and left in the middle of the night. Like Chirine, full of innocence, Sarah said, 'Yes, it's true,' and she told her about Cannes, Fat Joe, the boat to Tangiers with Didier, the shop that never materialized, the bidonville on the other side of the fence, her mother's boyfriends. The lady listened attentively with her pearly ears, and said, 'Okay, very good, thank you,' then she grabbed the little blonde girl and told her, 'Time to go, Camille.' Even though she was only ten, Sarah understood then that it was all the words' fault, it was always the words' fault; they'd put an end to her game of hopscotch as surely as a burst of gunfire, she should have kept her mouth shut. She was ashamed, and she stopped talking. The next time they went to the Cercle no one wanted to play with her; everyone knew she was the daughter of a whore.

Sarah went and perched next to Chirine.

'Your dad's a bastard,' she said, and took her hand. In *Marimar*, characters took other people's hands when they wanted to console them. Chirine shrugged her shoulders and sighed.

'No, that's just how he is. He's a man.'

All of a sudden they heard the growl of an engine; quickly, Chirine pointed to the path leading to the garage.

13

S HE'D BARELY STEPPED onto the lawn when she heard
the sound. The garage was further down on the right,
beyond another flight of brick-red steps that led down a slope
at the end of which Sarah would have seen some tools, a pile
of tyres, the Mercedes and maybe Driss on his motorbike.

'Tell him it's me who sent you down,' Chirine had said.
'Tell him we were upstairs together and he's got to take you
home.' But it was too late; the bike, at the bottom of the
slope, was already driving off. Driss was leaving. She'd have
to run very fast, faster than the motorbike. Sarah knew how
to run, how to get away from guys in the street, security men,
cops, school monitors during detention. But this was new:
this time she was the monitor, the cop stopping the wily kid
from getting away. But she was sure she could catch him up.
After all, that was all she did anymore—run after him.

Rather than turning towards the garage, she raced straight
to the door that opened onto the street, opened it without
bothering to close it behind her, and ran down the road.
There he was, a few feet from the garage entrance, shoulders

drooping, hair the colour of cinders, driving away. He vanished at the intersection. She ran, heels clicking one after the other on the asphalt, her breath quickening, the palm trees and villas receding; suddenly she was hit by the well-founded worry that she wouldn't be able to catch him up, it was impossible to catch up with a moving motorbike that was already out of sight, he was too far away already, his bike was too expensive, he'd never want a poor girl like her. 'If by the time I get to the junction I can't see him, that's it, I'm done, I'm giving up,' she thought to herself, now only a few feet from the corner where he'd disappeared.

But she didn't have time to give up. She was still running when he suddenly reappeared, flying into the junction to do a U-turn. He was coming back in the other direction and heading straight for her. He almost drove right into her—he braked only just in time. Sarah ducked to the right so abruptly that she tripped and fell face first, breaking her fall with her hand.

'Are you okay? Are you okay?'

He crouched down beside her and shook her shoulder—'I'm sorry, shit, I'm so sorry, I'm so sorry.' He didn't stop talking. 'I didn't see you, I wasn't expecting—I didn't think, I was driving, I was just driving along and…' She'd never heard him say so many words at once. She sat up slowly, pressing her scuffed knees on the asphalt and moaning slightly, though she wasn't really hurt. Once she got to a kneeling position she held out her hand; he took it without hesitating and helped her up. She didn't need him to, but at last she felt his soft skin against her raw, grazed hand, like a new piece of information that he was revealing about himself which she grasped hungrily—*the skin of Driss's hand is so soft*—and as she got up she held onto this skin with her fingers, and it was like a handshake that set in motion and finalized their future contract; a handshake that said, *deal.*

'Don't worry, I'm fine,' she said, brushing the dirt off her jeans.

'Are you sure? I didn't know, I didn't think you'd be here, running down the road. I was at Chirine's…'

Sarah stopped him. 'Will you give me a lift home?'

His mouth dropped open and he stared at her, his face pale, frowning, as if he was trying to understand a sentence in a foreign language. Then he jolted awake.

'Of course, yeah, sure, hop on.'

They crossed Anfa and then Aïn Diab, with its gated communities steps away from the sea, its clandestine bars in the back of vacant lots, and Sindibad, the amusement park by a field of sunflowers. On the side of the road a gigantic statue of the cartoon character, a smiling boy with a turban on his head and a bird on his shoulder, pointed to the entrance to the park. In the distance she could see the big wheel that sometimes got stuck. There were hawkers at the entrance selling *jabane*, pacing back and forth with their big wooden sticks wrapped in white nougat that was all sticky under the plastic protecting it from flies. For two dirhams, all toothless smiles, they sliced off chunks with small, sharp, sturdy knives. Sarah had never seen a *jabane* seller with teeth, but no one seemed to draw any conclusions from that, everyone carried on buying two-dirham slabs whenever they saw the wooden stick parading down the street. The entrance to Sindibad was black with people, veiled women with two kids in their arms being pushed aside by slum dwellers trying to slip through the railings before getting caught by the guards, the kicks and shouts—'Get out of here, you filthy pigs, I'm calling the cops, I'm going to send you straight to prison.' Kids from a local school threw themselves at a *jabane* seller who was slicing wildly with his knife, almost poking his own eye out; their teacher ran after them, panicked, yelling out their names one by one, Jawad, Tarik, Othmane, Nabil, Meriem. The sky was already a deep blue; smoke rose from the kebab stands, the smell of iodine wafted in from the sea, cars stuck behind crowds of beggars blared their horns; and over the whole scene floated chanting from the mosque.

'Straight?' shouted Driss, turning his head slightly.

She'd been telling him which way to go for a good ten minutes, and he still hadn't figured out she was sending him round in circles.

'Left,' she shouted.

Whenever he slowed down, trapped between two cars in unmoving traffic, or obeying a red light, Sarah would lean into his neck and inhale his cologne—it was the Giorgio Armani that everyone bought at Aïcha Parfumerie, the same as Kamil and some of the guys in her class wore. She'd smelt that fresh, salt-water, tangerine smell a thousand times. Turned out, she thought to herself, that for years she'd been smelling Driss.

'Stop here,' she said.

They'd reached the sea, the quiet end of the Corniche, not far from the mosque. Driss brought the bike to a standstill and looked at the waves breaking on the grey sand, the plastic bags drifting in the air with the pigeons, the empty water bottles rolling among the seashells.

'You live round here?' he asked.

There was nothing there but the road, the sea, the mosque and a plastic surgery clinic called The Plastic Surgery Clinic.

'Yeah,' she said, climbing off the bike. 'I live in the Atlantic.'

He looked at her curiously for several seconds. Then he smiled.

'Whatever.'

His face relaxed; Loubna's thyme leaves fluttered above his nose. He was still gripping the handlebars.

'You coming to Americano's?' asked Sarah. Without waiting for an answer she turned away from the sea and crossed the road. She heard the engine cut, then little steps hurrying to catch up with her.

14

YOU TOOK THE FIRST LEFT after the plastic surgery clinic then immediately turned right onto a small, treeless street, little more than an abandoned lot where young men came to hang out. On the other side was Americano's. You could smell the grilled meat from three blocks away. People stood waiting their turn as two bearded guys, the *chouay*, skewers in hand, took orders for kofta wraps, kebabs, chips and plates of merguez. There were three Coca-Cola-red plastic tables in front, but most people preferred to sit on the ground on the other side of the road. There was the glow of flames from cigarette lighters, people chucking dirty paper napkins at each other and rolling cans of Pom's on the parched earth. The evening might end in a fight, or a football game. Kamil used to come here sometimes at night—he said the meat was pretty great and he liked to hang out with real people. He always had flatbread baked with kofta and mustard sauce that he took back to his car and ate with the doors locked.

Sarah walked up to the front of the queue. Driss followed her. Generally, the people in the queue didn't dare kick up a fuss when she pushed in; they figured she must be the daughter of someone important. When she was with Kamil, it worked even better. The few times she'd been yelled at she yelled back, louder—'You'll see when I tell my father about this, arsehole'—and they shut up.

'What do you want?' she asked once they found themselves facing one of the bearded guys. There were bowls of sliced tomatoes, lettuce, red onion and parsley; behind him smoke rose from grilling skewers of meat and the other *chouay* plunged a basket of chips into a vat of boiling oil. Driss was standing with his arms crossed, looking around.

'Nothing,' he replied.

She ordered merguez and chips in a flatbread with ketchup and mayonnaise. It was handed to her a minute later, wrapped in white paper. Inside the bread the chips were soft and pulpy, bathed in sauce, just the way she liked them. 'Ten dirhams,' said the *chouay*. As she stuck her free hand into the back pocket of her jeans—it was empty—Driss started to squirm. 'No, no, you mustn't pay.' He pulled out a twenty-dirham note from his wallet, then led Sarah over to the side where the plastic tables were.

Since there were no free tables and Driss looked appalled at the sight of the people sitting on the ground on the other side of the road, she ate her sandwich standing up, facing him, the smoke from the grill wafting over her in waves. She took a greedy bite, got a scrap of white paper between her teeth, grimaced and wiped it off her tongue with the back of her hand. Sauce dripped down her chin. 'Wouldn't you rather eat it at home?' asked Driss between two silences, and Sarah answered with her mouth full, 'No, I like it here.'

When she'd finished, she screwed up the paper and dropped it to the ground, wiped her mouth and looked Driss in the eye. 'You can kiss me if you like.'

Driss's face didn't move. Even his eyelashes stopped twitching, and the thyme in his irises froze, as if the wind on the hills where it grew had suddenly dropped, as if the sauce in the tajine had stopped boiling and the sprigs of thyme in the meat stew had congealed. His eyes were empty. Sarah could have sworn no breath came out of his crooked nose or his clamped, petrified lips. It was like looking at a corpse. And then without warning he cleared his throat and came back to life.

'I don't know,' he whispered. 'I've never...'

Chirine had whispered to her at 17 Storeys, 'I don't think he's ever kissed a girl.' She said since they were teenagers he'd always come along to their shisha evenings but kept his distance at all times, playing patience while the others flirted. Even when his eyes were blinded by clouds of apple-scented smoke, he carried on playing cards. During a weekend in Marrakech two years earlier, Badr and Alain had shared a couple of whores in their hotel room, while Driss spent the days with Chirine sitting on a sunbed, a mint cordial in one hand, teaching her to play gin rummy.

'You just have to close your eyes,' said Sarah, 'and I'll kiss you.'

Driss's face froze again. It was surprising to see him par-alysed like this as though every new thing were a shock, but Sarah relished the right of life and death she had over him, this new feeling of power, when everything about her—the fact she was a woman, the fact that she was poor—had always condemned her to being dominated.

Driss revived. He closed his eyes. His lips quivered, as though he were holding back tears that might burst forth at any moment, pouring down over his cheeks, his neck, his stocky legs, the pavement. Sarah had to keep the street from being flooded. She moved towards him. He was barely taller than her, so she didn't need to stretch her neck or stand on tiptoe—she just had to take a step and lean forward. Which is what she did. She pressed her mouth to his still quivering lips. She stayed like that, patiently inhaling the aroma of black soap, argan oil, Giorgio Armani and chlorine; he definitely had the skin of a rich man. Only then did she move her lips, adding saliva, and she felt Driss's whole body convulse in panic, and his mouth was still stiff, paralysed by this trespass. She was going to have to use violence. Her tongue poked its way inside, pushing, doing battle with his teeth, and then once it was inside it colonized the entire space, his palate, the walls of his cheeks, his gums, each molar. She felt quite at home there now. As the offensive eased, his jaw relaxed and his tongue crept forward, very slowly, conquering every millimetre of the soft interior of her mouth, and she thought to herself, who cares about the slobber, the jerkiness, the fact I'm almost choking, because this slobber, this jerkiness, this choking all come from him, the richest man in Casa; even, perhaps, as rich as the king.

'Marriage certificate.'

The beam of a torch was trained on them. The light was so blinding they had to pull apart to cover their eyes; through her fingers Sarah saw the silhouette of a policeman in uniform, with a blue and white cap on his head and mayonnaise on his moustache. He held a plate of merguez sausages in his other hand.

'Marriage certificate or it's straight down to the station.'

Behind them, some guys sitting around the Coca-Cola tables laughed, showing parsley between their teeth. 'All right, all right, easy now,' said Driss, waving his hand to chase away the light. He said the words in Arabic, almost instinctively, as if he'd read the chapter in a travel guide, 'What to Do If You Get Arrested'.

'Wait here,' he said to Sarah, drawing the cop to one side. There was the smell of grilled meat, the guys sitting around the tables whistling and catcalling, 'Hey, petite, you're gorgeous,' sounds from the wasteland opposite, the Casa football team anthem. She felt the cold January wind, heard the soft clink of cans knocking against each other, insults, gobs of phlegm; and there was Driss. She watched him, a giant on stocky legs, one relaxed hand on the cop's shoulder, the other rummaging in his pocket for a hundred-dirham banknote, coming out with a knowing joke, the occasional wink; and the cop smiled back at him as he grabbed the banknote and slapped Driss on the back. Driss said, 'Go get yourself a merguez, Sidi, make me happy.' Driss, a giant among the poor, thought Sarah, Driss, the giant whom she'd just kissed. With all his money there'd be no more cops, no more law—just the two of them, that would be the law.

15

EVERY YEAR at the beginning of February, the country waited for rain, and the rain didn't come. So the king would call upon the faithful to pray. It was on the news: business leaders kneeling in the direction of Mecca alongside drivers and car attendants, rabbis, shoulders covered by their taliths, praying in synagogues, beggars in the Jewish cemetery, yarmulkes on their heads, reciting prayers among the graves. The presenter announced in Arabic: 'Communities are once more coming together to pray for rain.' And eventually every year around mid-March it did rain, and every year it was a miracle. The king gave a speech about God and the brotherhood of man, regardless of a person's name, religion, income, social status—Morocco walks hand in hand, he said. In the bidonville, kids stood in the rain getting soaking wet and splashing in the puddles, tilting their heads back to drink the raindrops, and in Sarah's living room Abdellah's mother wept as she watched the little television. 'Hand in hand,' she kept saying.

In mid-March 1994, just as every year after the prayers, it rained. On Beach 56, raindrops speckled the sand with shadowed dimples that made it look like the leopard skin coats that the mothers wore to pick up their children from private nurseries in the Triangle d'Or, except that poor kids were playing football on it.

Only crazy people swam in this weather. As night fell, the guys who were still at the beach made their way up to the road, panting slightly, their faces damp and their tracksuits sandy. Their trainers splattered Sarah and Yaya as they went past. 'Motherfuckers,' yelped Yaya, his face full of sand. He wiped his eyes with his fingers, then on the corner of the towel he was sitting on. 'I'm covered,' he said as he stood up. He handed the joint to Sarah and ran to rinse himself off in the sea.

She told him everything about Driss: the kiss outside Americano's a month and a half earlier, and the weeks that followed. 'And it doesn't bother you?' Yaya asked. She shrugged. 'Nope, I don't care.' The last six weeks Sarah kept hearing the question muttered behind her back, 'You think it really doesn't bother her?' At La Notte, Badr and Alain, seeing her sitting on a banquette with her arms draped round Driss's shoulders, cast each other perplexed glances. It was the same with the girls at the lycée, keeping one eye on this new couple as they kissed their partners during the slow dances. Married women, legs crossed, glass of wine in hand, nodded sagely—'Of course she's in it for the money'—then added, with a distracted air, their eyes fixed on Sarah's downy back in her new halterneck dress, 'I don't see how it doesn't bother her.' Maybe Driss's ugliness expanded next to her beauty, colonizing the space; maybe, now he had a young woman constantly on his arm, his biker's taciturnity, his stammer, his jittery demeanour, and his ungainly shuffle struck observers a little more sharply. No, it didn't bother her. When she said that to Yaya, he sighed. 'Come on, there's no way his money makes up for it.' She didn't have time to respond—it was right then he got sand kicked in his face and went to rinse his eyes in the sea. Lying on her towel, Sarah watched him kneeling in the shallows, splashing his face, and grumbling, 'Fuck, it's cold.'

Yaya had lost his brother to the sea. Sarah knew that because he'd told her an hour earlier on the Corniche, when she'd suggested going to sit at the beach and watch the rain. 'It makes me feel strange, the sea. I don't like it. It's where my brother's death happened.' He said it like that, talked about death like it was the rain, as if it had showed up in the bow of a wave, circumscribed in a specific place beyond which it no longer applied. There was no other way of describing this death because it wasn't true. His brother had been knocked over at six in the morning on the Aïn Diab road by a Bentley going at two hundred kilometres an hour. One of the Benchekroun sons. Yaya raged, 'I was just a kid, I wasn't earning money yet.' So his mother had accepted thirty thousand dirhams from the family on condition she didn't report it to the police. At the funeral she told the imam her son had drowned.

When Yaya came back and sat on the towel alongside Sarah, face dripping and eyes red with salt, he took the joint and said he'd just remembered that when he was there by the water a few months ago some jerks had stiffed him on a deal, some seriously good shit, and one of them was also a Benchekroun. It wasn't the same family, but that one had an uncle who knew the king, so Yaya couldn't do anything. 'Or I'd have smashed their faces in,' he said. 'I'd never let a rich bastard call the shots.' Sarah wanted to say, nah, you'd never have beaten them up; and you're wrong, it's always the rich bastards who call the shots. That was precisely the reason Driss's money was enough for her, and why his looks didn't bother her. Sitting in the rain on sand studded with cigarette butts, with the noise of gulls, screeching car horns on the avenue, insults flying back and forth between the footballers, Sarah would have loved to tell Yaya what she'd seen at Driss's house. Among all the lush vegetation, the marble bathroom, the huge windows with views over the whole city, the pool, there was something Yaya couldn't even imagine: calm. A calm worth ten times, a hundred times Driss's ugliness—an eternal calm that nothing could disturb apart from perhaps the distant, rhythmic music of a gardener's secateurs. Nothing, not a Bentley killing a kid as he crossed the road, not a debt, not the police. As long as there were banknotes in Driss's wallet, an inexhaustible supply of banknotes belonging to a man as rich as the king, wherever he lived, wherever she lived, there would be real calm: the end of injustice, domination, violence; the calm of a place where she could do whatever she wanted.

But Sarah didn't say this to Yaya. She picked up a small rock. 'You'll have to smash up the sea instead,' she said, and lobbed it into the Atlantic. Yaya laughed. He picked up a larger rock and did the same thing, his movement powered by all the violent rage he'd have galvanized if he'd been able to beat up those fuckers the Benchekrouns for real. Par for the course, thought Sarah. Soon she'd be surrounded by calm, but for him, violence was forever.

'You must be very happy, petite, now you've got what wanted from Driss,' Yaya said after a while.

The rain hadn't stopped, it was pitch dark, and Yaya was on his tenth rock. He really didn't get it. Of course she hadn't got what she wanted; she had to marry him now.

16

RIGHT AFTER THE KISS, while Driss was joking around with the cop, Sarah made her escape. Not like a thief walking off with some *aker fassi* from Aïcha Parfumerie—which he must never find out about—but like a lady, so much more elegant than anyone else at the kebab stand or the patch of ground over the road, even though her sweatshirt was covered in ketchup. She walked over to them, distinguished, a queen, with a spring in her step, a glorious shimmy. She floated along the pavement, gliding the way people do who have no need to run from anyone or after anyone. That was how she would walk towards him the day of their wedding, with a bouquet of white roses and a flock of little children holding up her train; that was how she would walk for the rest of her life.

The cop stared at her, dumbstruck. 'What does she want?'

'I have to go,' she announced. Driss, after a few seconds of facial rigor mortis, began to tremble; his breath grew ragged, his mouth twitched as he tried to utter sounds. The cop held his plate up to his nose: 'Have a merguez, it'll calm you down.' Then, in one breath, Sarah's argument flooded out of her—it was seven o'clock already, her father would be waiting for her on the doorstep. The father trick always worked. She had to go home on her own, and she had to go home now. As she spoke Driss's eyes narrowed and his eyebrows lifted like commas up to his creased forehead in an anxious grimace.

'You can give me the money for a taxi if you like.'

She closed her hand over the twenty-dirham note and gave him a quick peck on the cheek. 'Ooh la la!' cried the cop with his mouth full. And off she ran.

Two days later Karim picked her up from school and drove her over to Chirine's house. She walked in and asked Chirine for Driss's number. 'So you've done it, you've kissed!' yelped Chirine with a little skip, running upstairs to find her blue laminated address book covered in stickers shaped like flowers and musical notes. Sarah leafed through it, perched on a stool in the living room where two nights before she'd seen Chirine's mother in a beige djellaba. Chirine stood in the hall by the phone. She dialled a number and after a few moments said, 'Hey, it's Chirine, you're never going to guess what—Sarah's going out with Driss. No, I swear it's true,' she kept saying. As she wrote down the number on the back of her hand, Sarah imagined herself already married to Driss, imagined she was sitting in her own living room. All of it—the taffeta curtains, the taupe stool, the glass coffee table, the hardwood drinks cabinet—belonged to her. She'd come in from the pool to jot down some instructions for the staff. Sarah drank the orange juice the maid had brought her, but tasted the fine cognac she would sip from a crystal glass to unwind, her diamond ring glinting.

She left the red house, waving on the way out to Chirine, who was still on the phone and responded with a nod. Kamil was waiting for her outside. He dropped her at the call shop on Boulevard Zerktouni.

'Why don't you call from my place,' he said, 'I don't care about the money.' He was very pleased with himself because he'd paid Maroc Telecom to let him choose the six digits of his phone number: '007007, like James Bond, get it?' But Sarah refused. 'I don't want to come round to yours, I want to go to a call shop. Sorry, that's how it is.' She knew perfectly well the price she'd pay for calling from Kamil's: she'd have to take off her jeans, because they'd be standing by the bed; taking off her jeans was the price of everything, including the jeans, but she was faithful to Driss now. Kamil gave her money for the call anyway, and a bit extra to buy Tofita sweets and a packet of Marquise cigarettes.

The entrance to the call shop was blocked by a pile of gas canisters. A guy was doing round trips, picking them up one by one and carrying them on the back of a scooter. He wore a tee shirt, though it was quite windy—people were saying it was going to rain, even though the king hadn't ordered the prayers yet. Behind him, white letters on a blue background spelled out 'BALABAAK SERVICE—NEWSPAPERS—PHONE CALLS—DAIRY PRODUCTS—FRUIT AND VEGETABLES.' The red awning below the shop sign was printed with five La

Vache Qui Rit logos. Sarah walked in, past the cold drinks in the window to the left and the footballs in their plastic nets that hung around the door. She ignored the packets of crisps stacked up to the ceiling—not easy—and the pile of French magazines, November issues this time, not too bad. Once she'd had her fill of pizzas from Café Campus, milkshakes from Jus Ziraoui, and taxis, the first thing she always asked a boy for was a glossy magazine; she read the interviews with singers until she knew them by heart, until she could repeat whole sentences like songs on the two-hour walk to school in the morning; it was almost as good as having the Walkman that Kamil had promised her but had never got round to buying. She pawed the ground in frustration when she overheard scraps of conversation in the school gymnasium between the girls who could afford a decoder to watch pirated French television channels. Sometimes she heard the scoops weeks before she was able to read them in the next issue of the magazine, so when she finally opened it, leaning against the fence of the bidonville, every bit of information read and already known was a victory, as if her own mind had influenced the pages—as if she controlled the world.

But today in Balabaak Service Sarah had eyes only for the phone booth in the back. Its windows were so dirty that she could barely make out the grey telephone inside. She entered and slipped a one-dirham coin into the slot to get a dialling tone. Then she composed the six digits she'd written in ballpoint on the back of her hand.

'Allô.'

That was the greeting. When she heard the intonation, she knew it was the right number. It was allô pronounced Arabic-style, the weight falling on the final syllable instead of the lilting, polite, questioning intonation of the French allô. It was fierce, uttered like an insult—a snarl whose meaning was clear: 'Yeah, it's me, and what you going to do about it.' When Sarah asked to speak to Driss, she got no reply, she just heard the clatter as the receiver was dropped and then a shout, 'Telephone!' There was movement, a chair being shifted, footsteps on the stairs, a sneeze and then suddenly a new allô. Sarah thought for a moment she was going to faint. But it wasn't Driss. It was a girl's voice, saying, 'Hamza? Is that you?' Again, Sarah asked to speak to Driss, and again there was the clattering sound. The little gauge on the telephone clicked; she was going to have to insert another coin in a minute. Finally there was the sound of rustling and someone clearing his throat, and she heard Driss's voice.

'Allô?' With a rising intonation.

The greasy receiver almost slipped from Sarah's hands as she said, 'It's me, it's Sarah.' Driss said nothing. Between them, for several long seconds, there was no more than the metallic hum of the telephone line. She had nothing to lose. 'Are we going out together now?' she asked. He said, 'Sure, okay.' She asked if she could come over and, after a brief pause, he said yes. Sarah bought the sweets and cigarettes, then walked back out of the call shop to Kamil in his convertible.

He drove her to Anfa Supérieur and dropped her at the most beautiful villa in the whole of Casa. As she opened the passenger door she told him it was over, then she got out and rang the doorbell. That's how it began.

17

THAT'S HOW IT BEGAN, her discovery of Driss and all the Drisses of Morocco—with the way he opened the front door. Everything that was to come, all the violence and absurdity, was contained in that instant, the moment Driss himself chose to open the front door. The way he ran down the stairs as soon as he heard the doorbell so as to get there before the maid, the way he turned the handle with his sweaty hand, panting and pink-cheeked. He didn't say hello, he just muttered, 'This way, hurry up.' And then he led Sarah not into the house but out to the garden, casting anxious glances back towards the grand villa they were implacably walking away from, and she felt, with a clarity more intense than the midday sun on the square in front of the Hassan II Mosque, the silent strangeness of this distancing, the unease.

As she walked down the long slope of freshly mown lawn, still damp after being watered by the gardener who was now perching precariously at the top of a ladder, as she inhaled the scent of the hibiscus swaying in the wind that was surprisingly strong this evening, as the twenty-metre-long pool came into view at the end of the garden, perhaps Sarah already had an inkling of the challenges ahead that would begin as soon as she reached the pool, when her attempts to walk back up to the closed villa would be thwarted, this time and every time. Or perhaps not.

In any case, it didn't stop her.

At the end of the lawn there was a terrace of pale grey flagstones spangled with small needles the wind had shaken from the branches of a tall araucaria tree that swayed over the pool. 'The gardener will sweep them up,' Driss muttered, more to himself than to her, as though he too had only just discovered the effects of the squally late afternoon weather. He hadn't so much as glanced at Sarah—not when he opened the front door, not while he was leading her down to the pool; even when he surreptitiously turned his head to the right to check she was keeping up with him, his eyes slid over her, like they used to. He was compulsively kneading a set of keys between his fingers. At the pool he suddenly turned sharply to the left. And then Sarah saw it: at the end of a stone path a little bungalow nestled among the trees. 'It's so you don't have to go all the way back up to the villa after you've swum,' he said, still walking ahead, a tremor in his voice. He put the key in the lock, slid open the glass door, walked into the house—it was just one big room—turned on the lights and sat down, stiff and awkward, on a big grey sofa, not sure what to do with his long arms. Sarah remained standing in the doorway. She felt her cheeks grow hot, the blood pumping in her heart.

'I know that.'

They stared at each other, him sitting on the sofa, her still in the doorway, two metres away from him; she had to raise her voice to be heard over the whistling of the wind.

'Of course I know it's so you don't have to go all the way back up to the villa after you've swum.' The truth was she had no idea; she'd never seen a garden so big they'd had to build a second house by the pool, not at Badr's, nor Chirine's, not even in *Marimar* after she marries Sergio. She was wearing a pair of jeans from Paris like Chirine's, she'd made sure he'd seen her ten, fifteen times at Café Campus, full menu, Fanta, milkshake, double *ness-ness*; no one had ever seen her driver, but no one had ever seen her on the bus either. It was obvious she was French, beautiful, that boys liked her; people might know she skipped school and smoked kif, or find her solitary, mysterious, mean. But no one would ever guess she was poor; that was impossible.

And yet now here was Driss saying just that. He began to gabble, barely stopping for breath, like that time outside Chirine's when he'd virtually driven into Sarah on his bike and knocked her over, unleashing a flood of garbled apologies, 'I—sorry, I don't mean, I just thought like—your blue dress at Badr's place, you made it yourself, no watch, no jewellery, your trainers, sorry, I thought, well, I didn't think you'd know—I mean—things like that.'

There was a moment of hesitation. The language of money—Sarah hadn't imagined he'd speak it so well. Given how little he spoke, it surprised her to realize he'd learnt it perfectly when he was a child, it was his mother tongue, his first language, the language that dominated all his other languages, even before he'd learnt to speak. She hadn't expected to have to go into this feeling so exposed. She couldn't fool him; he could see.

She walked into the room and sat down next to him on the sofa without a word, close enough to smell the black soap and Giorgio Armani cologne on his skin. She stared straight ahead, in silence, like him. Somewhere a clock ticked. After a while he said, 'Do you want something to drink?' and she said, 'Yes, Pom's.' He got up to fetch a can of Pom's from the small open-plan kitchen behind them. There was another grey sofa, a table, a large green pool table and posters of Paris exhibitions on the walls; but Sarah just stared through the half-open glass doors, beyond which the pool trembled and the wind still blew. He came back with a tray, put it on the table and they each drank a can of Pom's and watched the needles falling from the araucaria. 'The gardener will sweep them up,' Driss said again.

Sarah put her empty glass on the table. She turned towards him, leaned her tanned terracotta face towards his ugly face, and kissed him. It was no better than the first time. As she kissed him—in spite of the slobbering and the stiff tongue jabbing the back of her throat—she took off her trainers, her jumper, her jeans, her panties. In stages, she taught him how to make love, occasionally bumping against the corner of the coffee table, forcing herself not to notice his crooked nose, pointy chin, greasy skin, sharp little teeth. She plunged into the melting green of the thyme and bay, melting into the beef tajines that Loubna would cook in their grand villa that would be filled with gold, tiaras and so many diamonds on the floor that people would trip over them. This time Sarah didn't pretend it was the first time.

When Driss offered later to take her home on his bike, she accepted. He said, 'What about your father?' She said, 'There is no father.' When they reached the bidonville, he started with surprise but said nothing. The truth established itself between them, like a needle blown by the wind onto a stone flagstone, that no one swept up.

18

A T SEVEN A.M. one morning in November 1993, an official of the port of New York blew his whistle as a brand-new cargo liner sailed into the terminal. It was windy that morning in New York, and the sea air stung his face. Turning towards the articulated trucks parked in the hangar behind, he made large circular motions with his arms. At this signal, one of the trucks drove onto the quay just as the ship's horn began to sound. It was a morning of harmony: the vehicle reached the dockside at the exact same moment the ship berthed. The port official looked up. Above the waterline the derrick swung into action; its huge arm plunged into the fog and was submerged. It reappeared a moment later, its cables firmly gripping a shipping container. It took one hour and twenty articulated lorries to unload the seven hundred and fifty freight containers one by one. Among them were three red containers that had travelled thirty days from Casablanca. Each one contained fifty thousand pairs of jeans, dispatched by Jean's Fabric, the largest clothing factory in Morocco.

Sarah and Driss were sitting at a plastic table at Crep'Crêpe. She was eating a waffle with Nutella and whipped cream while he explained to her that the derrick was like a crane, and the smell of iodine on the breeze was the same as it was here because it's the same ocean, and with every new detail Sarah stopped chewing, fascinated, and he could see in her open mouth pulpy chocolate pasted all over her teeth and tongue. Every so often a fly buzzed near her face and she waved it away in irritation. The moronic Crep'Crêpe manager turned up the sound on the little TV that hung in the corner above their heads.

'Turn it down,' she barked, and Bilal barked back, 'Shut your mouth, it's the king.' It was early February 1994 and the king of Morocco was calling the faithful to pray for rain, and Sarah did not care at all. She wanted to hear about America.

'What usually happens,' Driss went on, 'is the client gives the forwarder the bill of exchange guaranteed by the bank on receipt of the goods. But this time they didn't want to. So we've been fighting them since November.' The Jean's Fabric factory was in the building opposite Crep'Crêpe. It occupied six floors, each one seven hundred metres square, and there were two other factories in Sidi Moumen to accommodate the overflow. 'Twelve hundred workers,' Driss told her. He and his father shared an office on the sixth floor, but this afternoon they'd sent the company president to go and put the wind up the piece workers to get them to work harder. As soon as his father left the office, Driss went down to meet Sarah for a crêpe.

He met up with her whenever he could—after school, when she went walking on the beach, at Jus Ziraoui where he bought her milkshakes, in the call shop. Whenever they said goodbye, he'd stammer, 'Tomorrow? See you tomorrow?' And they'd fix a place to meet, and again the next day, and then again, and soon it was every day. Every day for the last two weeks Driss had picked her up after school, or left Jean's Fabric to meet her for lunch, just for an hour, wherever she wanted. Every day she chose Café Campus. He sat opposite her without speaking and watched her eat a club sandwich. He wanted to see her every day, but he didn't talk to her. He drove his monster of a bike that roared with all the country's anger; its roaring invaded every space, stopped all conversation, made people put their hands over their ears, made children cry—but he barely said hello to her and, after he did, he fell silent. Sarah didn't say anything either. She'd never had to talk to boys before, because of their constant jabbering, so she'd never learnt how. They ate seriously, listening to the clatter of Driss's knife slicing his cheese panini into six equal parts, and the sigh of air as Sarah held the ketchup bottle over her chips. They lifted their forks to their mouths and watched the pretty girls with sunglasses on their heads in the middle of winter, California style, and the waiters as they licked their greasy fingers after serving a pizza. Sometimes they cast one another a surreptitious glance, as if to check the other was still there, which mattered, after all, Sarah thought as she ate the last chips, because in their case being together literally meant being together, next to each other— that was all they needed. They smiled vaguely at each other, then Sarah mopped up some sauce with a piece of semolina bread, and Driss blew bubbles in his mint cordial through a straw. At the end of the meal Sarah said, 'Shall we go?' And they went.

They saw each other every evening at the little house by the pool, where they sat next to each other on the grey sofa and watched the water rippling; they listened to each other breathing. He drank Pom's and stared into space and she lay on her tummy on the floor, outlining in felt-tip pen the faces of stars in last year's magazines. She coloured the men's lips red then decided she was bored and began to undress. He gazed at her in astonishment. They made love, then it was over and neither of them said much—all she sensed, lying there with her cheek against his chest, was the beating of his heart and the squirt of Giorgio Armani cologne that he must have put on before she arrived. After a while someone shouted from the big house: 'Driss!' He stood up slowly, put on his jeans, his AC/DC sweatshirt, and walked back up the garden to the house, with his duck-like gait. Five minutes later he came back and said to Sarah, 'Let's go.' She was already dressed. They left and drove to Hay Mohammadi. When they got to her house, she said goodnight and pecked him on his cheek. He tensed and said, 'Tomorrow? I'm seeing you tomorrow, right?'

'Yes,' she said, 'See you tomorrow.' He relaxed and drove off, grinning like a kid.

Every weekend she spent hours watching him working on his bike in the garage, drinking orange Tang through a straw and sitting cross-legged on a pile of tyres. 'What are you doing?' she asked him from time to time. 'The brakes,' Driss mumbled. She sucked up the last drops of Tang then rummaged for another in the plastic bag from the *mahlaba* where earlier on he'd bought her four packets of Merendina and a strawberry-flavoured Raïbi drinking yoghurt. She emptied the little sachet of orange powder that smelt like boiled sweets into a glass and went to fill it from the rusty tap that spurted out water when she turned it on, then came back and perched on the tyres.

'What are you doing now?' she asked between sips.

'Still the brakes,' said Driss. One time, just to see, she lowered the glass of Tang and announced, 'Tomorrow night you're taking me to a restaurant, and you have to buy me a Walkman.' Driss carried on changing the brake pads without answering. But the next day, brakes now functioning, he took her to Boga Boga and after they sat down at their table, with its white tablecloth and plastic orchid, he handed her a Walkman, still in its box. She was ecstatic—this was way easier than it had been with Kamil. 'Oh wow, thank you!' she said, as she tore open the shiny blue box with the Sony logo and took out the metallic grey rectangle inside and held it, cold in the palm of her hand. Beyond excited at the earphones and the tapes of Madonna hits she'd have made at the Derb

Ghallef black market, she exclaimed, 'It's great, no?' Several seconds went by, like every time she said something to him. Driss frowned and looked confused, as if in the throes of some heated inner deliberation. Until eventually his answer fell, heavy and slow like the last drop of a milkshake from Jus Ziraoui, finishing its descent down the side of the plastic goblet as she tipped it over her open mouth: 'Yes.'

At La Notte people gave them odd looks, this strange pair of mismatched birds who sat on a banquette and watched the others dancing—when Badr paid for a magnum of vodka, he found them so still that he didn't dare offer them a glass. Sarah was drinking mint cordial, like Driss, and they sat there as if they were at the ballet, watching the rock and roll and slow dances; she could have been wearing a fur coat or a red cocktail dress like in *Pretty Woman*, a pair of opera glasses in a gloved hand, he could have been in a suit, admiring the pas de bourrée and saltos arrière. 'D'you want another drink?' Driss kept asking her, even when her glass was still half full. 'No,' said Sarah. 'I'm fine.' They ate at 17 Storeys afterwards, sitting alongside a group that heckled and teased them, called them Tic and Tac, Belle and Sébastien. 'Can't you peel yourselves apart?' Sarah laughed, and Driss scowled. 'We aren't stuck to each other, you know,' he muttered as he took a bite of pizza.

There were times when he got overheated too. He'd taught her that word, talking about his motorbike, and Sarah thought he might as well have been talking about himself, given the state he got into simply by talking. Someone somewhere would say the word motorbike, and he'd be filled with excitement, he'd start speaking very fast, as if afraid that he wouldn't be allowed to finish, he'd go into detail about the bodywork, the mechanics, point out the dates of purchase and resale, or when the next model was coming out. It could last half an hour. Eventually he caught his breath and stopped talking. His shoulders slumped and he lowered his eyes, as if a little ashamed of having given in to this outburst—and there was silence again, the thick, oily puddle of their silence. As well as the motorbike, Sarah discovered other subjects that triggered his overheating—Swiss army knives, Concorde, card games and, like that time at Crep'Crêpe, the port of New York. She mentioned them when she was bored, to distract herself, or she discovered them with a chance remark. Each time, it was such a spectacle she'd stop chewing mid-bite.

Every day they showed each other their new faces, and every day each new thing, each spasm, stunned them—it was like the endlessly repeated experience of encountering a stranger. One lunchtime at Café Campus, Sarah bit into a pizza and tasted the thyme of the motionless irises she saw on the still face in front of her, its rutted skin made of hundreds of tiny grey craters like the rocky landscape where the plant bloomed on arid mornings on the shore of the Mediterranean. She could watch it for hours, this silent, ugly face, because it was the whole world, and this world would soon be hers, set in diamond rings on each one of her fingers.

19

S HE'D GOT OUT OF SCHOOL an hour early, at lunchtime, because her bastard of a history teacher had caught her chewing tutti frutti Bubbaloo gum. She was staring through the window at a group of little princesses lounging on a bench in the playground with their new handbags and, distracted, she'd blown a big bubble. 'That's it, Sarah, out!' bellowed the teacher. As she zipped up her pencil case, he muttered, '*Kassoula.*' Which meant dunce, useless, and she was enraged at being called that, even if it was better than being called 405 Mazout, the nickname for Hakim, the fat kid at the back of the class, who was so slow to recall capital cities they called him after the old Peugeots the kids' drivers were given. Now she sat and waited for Driss outside Café Campus. It wasn't her choice to wait outside, it was the stupid waiter's. He didn't want her to come in on her own. It wasn't done for a girl to sit in a restaurant on her own, he said, it gives a bad impression. 'I don't want any trouble with the cops.'

Sarah lost her temper. 'When Kenza Bennani comes in

to do her homework after school, you never worry anyone's going to take her for a whore.'

'Kenza Bennani's not the same,' he sniffed. 'Her father's a businessman.' He was quite unmoved by the fact that he'd served Sarah pizza ten times in the last two weeks alone, with Driss quite obviously sitting opposite her. 'I've seen you with so many different guys, how am I supposed to know if you're still with the one from the jeans factory?'

When Driss found Sarah smoking a Marquise outside the café in the cold, he went marching up to the waiter. 'Next time you let her in,' he stammered, staring up at him—the bastard was twenty centimetres taller—and tapping the floor with his foot. 'If I ever hear you've thrown her out, you'd better watch your back.' The man apologized profusely, bowing so deeply he was practically bent double. 'Excuse me, Sidi, pardon, I didn't know she was with you.' Sarah muttered, 'I don't want to stay here anyway,' and they went off to eat snails.

There were shacks selling snails all over Casa, but Sarah's favourite was at the back of the *jouteya* in Derb Ghallef. They walked through the alleyways of the souk, past endless little covered stalls selling fake Louis Vuitton bags piled up next to collections of lamps, counterfeit luxury watches, televisions and decoders for pirating French TV channels. Sarah and Driss had to get down off the bike, the alleyways were so crowded, and they made their way excruciatingly slowly behind fathers from Anfa who'd come to get their video players fixed and kids carrying change from an electronics shop to the book-seller. Sarah stopped every hundred metres. The guy selling Gucci baseball caps called to her, 'Lalla, my pretty gazelle, come in and try one, top quality caps, American quality!' Driss bought her a red cap and she stuck it on her head and went in to the guy selling satellite dishes who snoozed all day long, sitting on a stool surrounded by satellite dishes that lay open like huge grey hibiscus flowers swaying to the rhythm of his snores. 'Look at them dancing,' she said to Driss. It was said there were nine hundred and ninety-nine stalls in Derb Ghallef.

The snail stall wasn't easy to find. It was hidden away on Rue El Basra, not far from the hospital and a public high school. Girls in white tunics came rushing out, clutching tatty old textbooks with half their pages falling out while they waited for the bus. You could smell the green aniseed from the other end of the Derb. The stallholder scooped a ladleful of snails from a huge pot of boiling water spiced with rosemary and aniseed that sat on a stand fashioned from scrap metal, and poured them into bowls. At lunchtime there was a jostling crowd of customers. Sarah and Driss bought a couple of dozen snails and sat down against the wall to pick out the flesh with a big pin. 'How do you know this guy?' asked Driss. 'Because of the hospital,' Sarah said.

One night three years ago they'd gone to Morizgo at two o'clock in the morning. That's what everyone called the Ibn Rochd hospital because it was founded by Maurice Gau back in the days of the French protectorate, and it was called that up until independence. It was a big hospital like in the movies, low white buildings set around a lawn, an entrance for cars, way better than the lousy clinics you found in small towns or the faith healers in the countryside. 'May God help you,' said the taxi driver when he dropped them at the entrance—he didn't even let them pay. Monique had come home covered in blood; she'd been beaten up by the guy she was seeing.

There were so many sick people in the Morizgo waiting room they were practically sitting on top of each other, people were howling in pain, dropping their crutches, it was bedlam. But once you got to see the nurse, it meant the bedlam was nearly over, because then it was just a question of getting the hell out of there. There were only forty beds—metal ones with thin mattresses—and not enough doctors, ten stethoscopes that got passed around from room to room, empty cupboards, pills scattered all over the unwashed tiles, women writhing in agony before giving birth on the filthy floor. There were new mothers sleeping on blankets folded into four next to their babies because they knew no one was going to look after them, some had come specially from the countryside on an ONCF train in third class, and they had nowhere else to go. After the consultation Sarah sat in the corridor next to Monique, who was holding a compress to her eye—she couldn't open it because it was too swollen from the impact. The nurse thought her cornea might have been damaged. A nurse had cleaned her face with Betadine and dressed it with plasters. But she couldn't do anything for her eye. She needed antibiotics and anaesthetizing eyedrops, and some ointment.

'We don't have that here,' the nurse said to Sarah, 'we don't have the money for all the stuff we need. If you want to help your mother, you'll have to go and buy all this at the out-of-hours pharmacy next door.' It was two hundred dirhams. The pharmacist wouldn't give them a discount. 'Everyone comes straight from the hospital and asks me for free stuff, young lady; if I did it for you, I'd have to do it for everyone, and I'd be ruined.' Sarah went back to the Morizgo corridor and sat down on the floor next to Monique. They waited for the time to pass. At dawn they left and came upon the snail shack in Rue El Basra.

20

T HE THIRD WEEK it was pastries. Monique pounced on the box when she got back. 'Where did you get these?' she asked, her eyes shining, a corne de gazelle already melting in her mouth. 'Abdellah and his mother will be very happy.' Crumbs spilled into the gap between her breasts, which looked even bigger than usual in the low-cut purple jersey top she'd put on for the occasion. She was wearing mauve lipstick. It was almost dark.

Abdellah and his mother were indeed happy when they arrived and saw the *ghribas* and the honey cigars on the table in the living room. '*Hayhay*, you've gone all fancy on us,' said Abdellah's mother, as she sat down on the sofa and slipped a morsel of *chebakia* into the mouth of the baby at her breast. Abdellah grinned and sat down on the floor a couple of feet away from the radio, as he always did when he came over to listen.

'It's thanks to that little husband of hers,' he said, nodding towards Sarah.

'Better hang on to him then,' said his mother.

He was right, Abdellah, the pastries did come from her little husband. That's what he'd started calling Driss after seeing him bring Sarah back on his motorbike every evening for the previous three weeks—'Your little husband.' That evening, an hour earlier at sunset, he'd spotted the box through the fence as Driss handed it to Sarah. 'Take it, it's for tonight,' he'd whispered, but Abdellah hadn't heard. He also hadn't spotted it was from Bennis, the best bakery in Casa. But if he had seen the logo and heard the words, he might have understood before Sarah did what the pastries signified—he was smart, Abdellah, and his daily attempts to sell Flash Wondermint by tapping on the windows of Porsches stuck in traffic jams had given him a subtle understanding of what might be going through the mind of a rich man. Sarah didn't realize there was anything special about the pastries. They didn't seem any different to her than the gift of the Walkman in the second week, or the Gucci baseball cap she never took off, at home, at the Café Campus, even in the little pool house where they saw each other every evening. 'Why don't you sew that bloody cap onto your head while you're about it?' said her mother whenever she saw her. But the pastries weren't like the baseball cap.

Sitting between her own mother and Abdellah's, the two of them squirming with impatience and eating the little sweetmeats with their sticky fingers, Sarah couldn't eat a thing, not a crumb. It wasn't that she'd eaten too much at Café Campus that lunchtime with Driss—she hadn't even ordered a milkshake. It was because this evening was the Night of Doubt. In a few minutes a man on the radio was going to deliver his verdict, and it risked instantly putting her lunches with Driss at Café Campus in jeopardy. In Casa, Marrakech, Tangiers and every other town and city in Morocco, everyone had found a radio to listen to. The families in Anfa Supérieur even invited their maids and gardeners to join them on the sofa in the living room to listen to the news. In downtown cafés people squeezed round tables to listen to the radio that sat on the counter and hissed, 'Shut up!' if someone spoke too loudly in a fit of enthusiasm while the adverts were on—the Arabic jingle for Biscolaty biscuits that went on for a minute and a half, the French one for Judor lemonade that went, 'Judor, the golden drink with the golden glints.' A waiter snaked between the tables, teapot in hand, filling tea glasses and murmuring, 'It's on the house.' Taxi drivers double parked on the boulevards and turned up their car radios; a few even let street kids pile in and squash up on the back seat to listen. As soon as the programme's theme tune began, everyone's face froze with apprehension. In the cafés, in the houses in Anfa, at Badr's and Chirine's, in Zineb's cramped living room in the middle of town, in taxis, all the way to the ramshackle house where Monique and Sarah lived in Hay Mohammadi, everyone held their breath. The Minister of Habous and Islamic Affairs was about to announce the date when Ramadan would begin.

If there was a crescent moon in the sky, the fast would begin the following day, 11th February; Sarah was sure that was what was going to happen. She sat distractedly pressing the buttons on her Walkman, praying the moon wouldn't be visible and Ramadan wouldn't begin until the day after. 'Stop with that clicking, for heaven's sake,' snapped Monique, trying to grab the Walkman out of Sarah's hands. It was only a difference of twenty-four hours, but twenty-four hours is twenty-four hours, and two meals in a restaurant and two milkshakes as well. Driss, as he did every year, was going to pretend to his father he was fasting, which meant no more lunches at Café Campus, no freshly squeezed juices after school, no Boga Boga in the evening or late-night snacks at Crep'Crêpe—and the thought horrified her.

'I'd rather it began tomorrow, that way it'll be over sooner,' said Monique.

'Tomorrow? Are you crazy? It's obvious you don't fast, because I tell you what, we don't want it to begin tomorrow, we need the extra day to get ready.'

'You're such a hypocrite, Maman, it's not like you're going to be fasting, because of the baby.'

'And what about you, Abdellah? Are you planning on fasting?'

'Course I am.'

'Of course you are. Every year you stink of cigarettes.'

'Cigarettes? What cigarettes? Of course I fast, ask Sarah, *yak*, don't I fast? Tell them I fast!'

'Oh shut up, all of you!' Sarah cried as the adverts ended. The theme tune started and then it was the presenter's voice greeting listeners. Silence fell in the living room as, word after word, the verdict took shape: *Today, 10th February 1994,*

at 7.15pm, the Minister of Habous and Islamic Affairs transmitted the following communiqué to RTM...

The presenter didn't even have time to read the communiqué before the news broke over the city: the siren rang out. It flooded Hay Mohammadi, the Carrières Centrales, it might even have sounded as far away as Jean's Fabric in Sidi Moumen. And as though in response, other sirens began to ring out from other mosques in Casa, the mosque on the beach, all of them in harmony with mosques in other cities, Oujda, Laayoune, like wolves howling at the moon. In Tétouan, from behind the walls of the Jbel Dersa citadel that overlooks the entire city, came cannon fire, whose echo, it was said, could be heard across the entire Rif. And in the bidonville, women began to ululate on the other side of the fence. It was now—Ramadan had begun.

Sighing deeply, Abdellah and his mother went home – they had to prepare the next morning's *shour* to eat before the sun came up and the fast began. They took the remaining pastries with them. Monique insisted—'Have them tomorrow, go on, it'll make me happy.' She'd made sure before they left to tuck three *makrouds* into the palm of her hand that she scoffed in her bedroom behind the closed door. Sarah lay down on the sofa. There were damp spots on the ceiling, just like at Moustache's shop where she'd go back tomorrow for a tuna tomato sandwich on credit. She'd sneak upstairs at the pool café to eat it among the dealers, staring through the window at the little rich girls on their way to Café Campus, where in a slightly affected murmur they would tell the waiter they had their periods, so he could take their order without fearing God or the cops, because if the cops showed up they'd be happy to repeat the information and that meant he wouldn't go prison. Flattered to be let into their confidence, his qualms soothed, and unconcerned at the thought of serving the same girls thirty days in a row, with a knowing wink he set down on the table paninis and pizzas that were once again too expensive for Sarah. She didn't know if it was that thought that made her suddenly shiver, or the roar of the motorbike on the alleyway outside. Confused, she got up and opened the front door. There stood Driss in the dark. He was back.

'Hi.'

Behind Sarah, the bulb in the living room flickered. It was as though it kept switching Driss's eyes on and off; they went from being invisible to being windows onto the ridges of the High Atlas. She didn't immediately notice that he was holding another box of pastries from Bennis. She saw only thyme, fresh thyme that, even if it wasn't real thyme in a tajine, even if it didn't assuage her hunger, nonetheless promised her it would. It consoled her. Driss held out the box to her.

'Take it.'

'But you just gave me some,' said Sarah when she saw the logo.

Driss took a deep breath. His chest swelled, his lips trembled—he was overheating.

'It's for tomorrow's iftar,' he burst out, 'if you want to invite Abdellah and his mother to break the fast, the baby too, maybe other people, but there won't be enough if you invite other people, I can bring you more, you have to tell me how many boxes you need and I'll bring them over before iftar, you'll have to call me from a phone booth, and you can tell me how many boxes, if lots of people are invited, and if you don't want to invite lots of people you can give them to Abdellah and his mother, they'll like that, but maybe you'll want some for yourself, I'll bring another box for you and your mother, lots of boxes, call me and tell me how many and I'll bring them over.'

As he spoke, Driss fumbled in the pocket of his leather jacket. He drew out a hundred-dirham note and held it out to her.

'That's for tomorrow, for Café Campus, if you want lunch, even if I'm not there, it's enough for a pizza, a *ness-ness*, a milkshake, phone calls if you need to ring anyone, fruit juices, smoothies, I don't know if it'll be enough but we can see each other tomorrow before iftar, or after, whenever you prefer, you can tell me if it's enough, I'll come and find you here and you'll tell me if you need more than a hundred dirhams, if you do I'll give you a hundred and fifty, two hundred, whatever, just let me know, and if you want magazines I'll get you some more, you have to tell me when I come, before or after iftar, you choose, you have to tell me, money and pastries, how much you need.'

That was when Sarah realized. Back when she was with Kamil, after every date on the back seat of his convertible or at the villa in Dar Bouazza, she always went home utterly exhausted from the effort of alternately pleasing him and lying to him, even though ultimately they were one and the same thing. It used up all the energy she got from the milkshakes he bought her. She had to flatter his male vanity, pass off her misery as being feminine demands, rather than just being poor, which meant her life was completely dependent on him even though nothing was ever said. But in the silence between her and Driss, everything was said and he assented to it all.

2 1

YAYA HAD VANISHED. After Ramadan began she searched for him everywhere, every day. The second the bell rang at the end of class she grabbed her backpack, raced out of the classroom up the stairs of Building K and out of the school gates, where all the cars with their drivers sat waiting, bumper to bumper. She kept running, knocking into students idly smoking cigarettes outside the gate, crossed Boulevard Ziraoui at a hundred miles an hour, turned down Rue Sediki—more than once she was almost knocked down by a bus—until she got to the pool café, gasping for breath. Six pairs of heavy-lidded eyes looked up as she burst in— the kif smokers, slouching comatose on the metal chairs in Haroun's café, dissolving with hunger, thirst and the urge to smoke. But every day, behind them, the table at the back where Yaya scarfed down his endless cans of tuna remained vacant. Sometimes it was worse—someone else was sitting there. Sarah would be swept by a feeling of mad happiness immediately followed by intense disappointment. It reminded her of the time when she was little and she saw a soldier at the market, dark-skinned like her—her father. She ran to him, arms outstretched. The man looked baffled as he watched her approach. Her mother grabbed her arm. 'That's not your daddy,' Monique whispered, 'it's just a soldier.' It took a moment for Sarah to recover from this heart flip; for years after, the shock returned in waves, like ripples in a pond, whenever she saw army fatigues. Yaya's vacant table had the same horrible effect.

She refused to lose heart. She set off again, running over to Rue Al Kabir where she thought might find him squatting on the pavement between the traffic light and Jus Ziraoui. She clutched the hundred-dirham note in her hand as she ran, planning what she was going to say. 'Guess where I'm taking you!' Or, 'Wanna grab a bite at Café Campus?' like in an American movie, waving the banknote in his face. He'd say, 'No way, you're having me on,' before patting her on the back and telling her, 'I like your style.' Obviously, Café Campus would never serve Yaya during the month of Ramadan. 'The French girl can eat, but not you, get out,' the waiter would say. And the two of them would bait him: 'Fuck's sake, you can't force him to fast, how do you even know he's Muslim, maybe he's Jewish, what do you know about him, you can't do anything in this shitty country.' She knew perfectly well it wouldn't get them anywhere, the waiter would never take an order from an Arab-looking guy in the middle of Ramadan, but it made her laugh to think of them raising hell in the middle of the café. Then Sarah would order two pizzas and they'd eat them out of sight on the patch of wasteland behind the driving school on Rue Djila. Maybe some old lady would walk past and start yelling, 'Infidels! Police! Infidels!' and try to hit them with her cane, maybe a street cop would come running after them blowing his whistle. They wouldn't care—they'd run even faster, their teeth smeared with tomato sauce. That's how it was going to be, every lunchtime, with Driss's money.

But there was no one on the pavement on Rue Al Kabir. No one.

'Where's Yaya?' she asked Haroun at the pool café after four days of searching for him. He shrugged.

'No idea. Tunisia, maybe?'

She went up to the first floor and ate her pizza on her own, like before. It was much nicer than Moustache's revolting sandwiches, so that was progress, of sorts.

There was even more honking of horns than usual in the streets of Casa. On her way home from school, stuck in a traffic jam, the taxi driver rolled down the window—it was only February, but he said he was roasting to death in the heat. With an elbow sticking out of the open window, he stared at her curiously in the rear-view mirror. He whistled to attract her attention. Sarah felt his stare, but she ignored him, keeping her eyes fixed on the women in silk hijabs sitting in the back of their Mercedes and sighing at being stuck in traffic, or the men genuflecting on the pavement who'd been praying for rain for the last three weeks. She knew the taxi driver was about to say something. And he did.

'What's a girl like you doing in Hay Mohammadi?' Sarah smiled—lately all the taxi drivers had been saying that. Maybe it was her baseball cap, or the confident way she hailed a taxi, knowing the precise number of dirhams in her pocket, or the nonchalant way she sat in the back looking out of the window at the street rather than keeping her eye on the meter that made her look rich, at last; or maybe they simply smelt the thyme on her.

Sometimes cigarette smoke wafted in through the window and the driver would start honking furiously at the religious men kneeling on the pavement. 'Someone's smoking,' he'd yell. 'Which idiot is it? Where is he? Someone should give him a hiding!' Then the cars would begin inching forward again and he'd forget about it.

When she got home, Sarah drank the juice she'd hidden under her jacket. Around eight o'clock she heard the motor-bike draw up.

2 2

A BOY WHO DOESN'T TALK is infinite. Over time he could become a thousand different boys—maybe a soldier or even a Sergio with a hacienda. Week after week, during the month Morocco was sleeping, in the shadowy interior of the little house, Sarah studied Driss, trying to make him out; while he, over glass after glass of Pom's, was becoming increasingly at ease with her. Now he almost never asked, shoulders tensed, if they were going to see each other again the next day.

Every night he fell asleep beside her on the grey sofa, knocked out by the iftar sweetmeats. Sometimes his slumbering body jerked, as if he were afraid of sleep. She studied his features, hewn by violence, the big nose above the thin lips, and she saw the face of a friend; sometimes she stroked his forehead with the tip of her finger as he snored. When he woke up, around an hour before midnight, he didn't want her to leave—diffidently, he'd say, 'Shall we play cards?' His favourite card game was Mille Bornes. When he took the game out of the cupboard, he always went out of his way to point out that he didn't particularly like Mille Bornes, he preferred serious card games, intellectual ones, or games of memory, but this time—just for fun—they could play Mille Bornes. He always forgot he'd said that the night before and the week before, so they regularly found themselves sitting on the cold floor in the little house collecting milestones. Sarah cackled with laughter whenever she made him slow down with a 'speed limit' or an 'out of petrol' card, while he grew anxious and panicked at the thought of losing or not being able to move ahead. One evening as she snuggled up to him, she wondered out loud what would have happened if in real life they had travelled as far as they had in Mille Bornes. 'We'd have reached the end of the world by now,' she said. 'No,' he said, 'not the end of the world. But we'd have gone to New York three times.'

He knew the names of all the constellations, Ursa Major, the Whale, Andromeda. And he loved his watches; sometimes when Sarah went to dip her feet in the icy swimming pool, Driss stayed inside at the pool table, taking his Rolex apart under the ceiling light with a series of tiny screwdrivers; he peered at the cogs with a magnifying glass, removing the dial, the winder, the jewel bearings. He taught her new words. Sarah didn't understand anything about the anchor or the balance wheel, but she too, if she'd known how, would have checked if the watch could keep up with the passing of time; you can't trust anyone or anything in this life. Driss wanted to know everything about time, and the weather too. Every evening he wrote down in a little notebook the following day's forecast.

He also recorded nightly readings of both his barometer and his thermometer. He liked to predict and calculate. It must be so loud inside his head, thought Sarah—maybe that's why he likes silence so much. During evenings with Badr, Alain and Chirine, when the volume of laughter and music rose beyond a certain level, he stiffened, like someone who's seen a wasp and is afraid of being stung. And if, fortuitously, the laughter and music simultaneously died away, leaving a moment of silence hanging, his muscles visibly relaxed. Then someone would start talking again almost right away, and he'd shudder with fear, as if he had plunged so deeply into his inner turbulence that he had forgotten where he was.

All the night clubs were closed during Ramadan, and you couldn't go to people's houses either, because even though most of their parents didn't properly observe the fast, they were afraid of what the neighbours would think. So the group of friends didn't go out much. Sometimes they'd gather at Alain's, because he lived on his own in Gauthier; it wasn't as good as going to a villa in Anfa Supérieur, but he had a mezuzah on the front door so he could party and drink alcohol as much as he wanted. Every time Badr pressed the button in the lift, he'd say, 'I'd hate to live on top of other people like this.' Actually, for a middle-class Jew, Alain was doing pretty well for himself. The loan he'd taken out to buy his Audi was a bit of shock to his finances, so to make up for it he'd sorted himself out an excellent set-up: he rented a three-bedroom flat cheaply from a doctor, a colleague of his father's. He didn't speak to his father anymore, because of the drugs, but also because he resented his old man for having become a paediatrician instead of going into business like everyone else. That was why Alain hadn't wanted to go to university—look where you end up if you start studying, he always said. Even before he'd taken his baccalaureate he'd begun working in property with one of his rich Jewish friends. He was making decent money, but it wasn't Anfa Supérieur; what's more he knew perfectly well it never would be Anfa Supérieur, thanks to his moron of a father who wanted to heal all the starving people in the world.

One evening Badr sat eating a sandwich, enveloped in the cloud of black smoke that Alain, lolling on the sofa, had just exhaled. Badr declared he couldn't wait for Ramadan to be over so they could go back to hanging out in decent places. Alain was affronted. 'What's your problem, you fucker?' he said, spilling half his whisky. 'Why don't you go find yourself another Jewboy to cover for you during your Ramadan, hypocrite.'

Chirine, exasperated, muttered, 'It's okay, Alain, he was only joking.' It wasn't the first time she'd been short with him lately. Two nights before, he'd put on some music and asked her to dance and she'd refused. She was sitting with Sarah and Driss now. Visibly upset, she shook her head slowly, and then said, 'He's twenty-four, come on, how old's he going to be when he finally decides to get married? Twenty-eight?'

'That's the last time I'm inviting you over,' Alain muttered drunkenly, his voice slurred.

'Fine,' said Badr. 'We can go to Sarah's next time, she's French.' Before Sarah had a chance to come up with an excuse, Driss had already answered on her behalf.

'No way. Her old man's really strict.'

23

I<small>T WAS EIGHT IN THE MORNING</small>. Sarah was lacing up her trainers before she left for school when her mother burst into the living room.

'Tell me, does your little husband pay for all this?'

Monique was never usually out of bed before midday. Her fine hair stood up on end and the smudged kohl under her eyes reminded Sarah of when that guy put her in the hospital at Morizgo. 'Yeah, he does,' said Sarah.

'Tell him I want to go to Sidi Abderrahmane. I can't stand this anymore.'

Sidi Abderrahmane. Sarah thought her mother was going a bit far, but it was true she'd been complaining with increasing intensity since the beginning of Ramadan. All the Moroccans she usually went out with told her, 'Not during the holy month,' and there were no bars or night clubs open after sundown, not even a shisha café where she could hang out with the French men from the Cercle. There were maybe two or three men around who were single or not afraid of being caught by their wives, but every year it was the same frustration, and every year the same refrain: 'I can't cope with my life anymore. I can't stand it. I want to go to Sidi Abderrahmane to find a solution. Yes, I want to go, I'm telling you I want to go, I've made my decision. I just don't have the money. I don't have the two hundred dirhams to pay for it.' And every year after the end of Ramadan, the love affairs started up again, and Monique forgot she'd ever wanted to go there.

At first, Sarah didn't have the nerve to bring it up with Driss. A few months before, she'd driven past it in Kamil's convertible and asked if he'd ever been there. 'Sidi Abderrahmane?' said Kamil, nearly choking on his Coca-Cola. The liquid spurted out of the straw. 'Are you off your head or something?' He wiped his mouth with the back of his wrist. 'I'm not a crackpot!' But every morning Monique appeared in the living room and started plaguing her again: 'Well, have you asked your little husband yet?' Sarah couldn't stand it any longer. One evening at the little house they were sitting and staring at the reflection of the moon as it skimmed the dark surface of the water.

'Will you take my mother to Sidi Abderrahmane?'

Driss's cheeks grew pink when she said these words; she thought he might be about to choke like Kamil had, and she kept her eyes on the pool as she waited for his reaction. She felt his eyes on her. Eventually, he said, 'Okay.'

The following Saturday they drove down the coast on Driss's motorbike to Aïn Diab, with Monique following in a taxi. It was a little white island floating in the Atlantic a few metres from the shore, but all the way from the other end of the Corniche you could see the waves crashing on the rocks and the white limewashed walls of the jumble of houses perched one on top of the other. Monique got out of the taxi and stood on the tarmac. She breathed deeply as she gazed at the steps that wound past the little coloured doors all the way up to the tomb of the saint Sidi Abderrahmane. She smiled.

'I'm going to be rich.'

She crossed the road and stepped portentously onto the beach. Keeping up a constant chatter, she wandered through the little market where stallholders were selling candles, incense, pendants in the shape of Fatima's hand and miniature copies of the Koran the size of a box of matches. Driss bought her everything she pointed to.

'I'm going to be rich,' she kept saying, 'I'm telling you, they're all at it, the rich wives, then they lie about it, they say, "Ooh, it's *haram*, it's a sin, I'd never do that," but I'm telling you they're all at it, that's how they got to be where they are.'

Sarah said nothing. She just wanted the whole rigmarole to be over. She stared at the shingle, then glanced down the beach towards the little dock, where a gathering crowd indicated it was high tide. At low tide you could walk to the island knee-deep in water, but at high tide you had to pay five dirhams each way to get across, sitting on a large worn Pirelli tyre with a wooden plank nailed to its underside. Ten dirhams was affordable, it was everything else that was expensive—what that was, of course, depended on the witches' instructions. All over the island, down every alleyway, in tiny rooms, *chouafates* charged not by the quarter hour but by the minute, sometimes even by the word. In front of every door were trays filled with rolls of lead to be melted down to ward off the evil eye. If requested, they read tarot cards and palms. At the end they gave their clients all sorts of things to do, from burning clothes to sacrificing a black cockerel and casting it into the sea, which was practical as much as anything else, because the people who lived on the little island were the poorest of the poor, and afterwards they sent their children onto the reefs to salvage the slaughtered fowls for supper. Though Sidi Abderrahmane was very beautiful, it reeked, what with the lead fumes, fire and chalk, the moaning beggars squatting beneath the blue-painted shutters and the headless cockerels; on the sand down on the shore were animal skins, the bloody pelts of sheep and cows. Sarah had never seen these things up close; Abdellah had told her all about it. He said he didn't believe in any of that bullshit, it was mental, he wasn't scared of it, and Sarah said, laughing, 'Let's try it then, if you're not scared,' and he went as pale as the whitewashed walls.

Driss gave Monique ten dirhams for the return journey and two hundred for the sorcery consultation, the possible purchase of a cockerel and the price of the *fkih*, the religious man who would slit its throat. He walked her to the dock, helped her onto the tyre, which barely stayed afloat under her weight, and watched until she arrived safe and sound on the other side, flinching when a wave hit her full in the face and she almost fell in the water and drowned. He only breathed again once she'd set foot on the rock, soaked from head to toe, and hauled herself up the stairs to the tangle of little alleyways. Then he sat down on the sand. Sarah followed him obediently, though it unsettled her to be here among the destitute island families who didn't even have electricity and had to keep warm with car batteries, while at sunset the *chouafates* went home to their apartments in the city. Sarah was hungry, but since it was Ramadan there was no one on the beach selling bowls of bean soup or steaming *harira*, so she said nothing so as not to think about it, sat next to Driss waiting for her mother to finish and listening to the cries of the stallholders selling amulets and the screech of the cockerels just before they were slaughtered. Sometimes the sound of women weeping too. Apparently married woman who couldn't get pregnant came to stay for three nights in one of the little houses on Sidi Abderrahmane and nine months later they gave birth; the truth was that a *fkih* raped them every night to cure them, for as often as not it was the husband who was infertile. The women didn't dare tell anyone and lived with the shame and the *fkih*'s child until they died—Kamil was right, the people who came here really were crackpots. That's what Sarah told Driss: her mother was crazy and this place was for crackpots.

'I like it,' he said.

He began to overheat, his breath grew short and he got carried away at certain words, almost drowning out the cries of the cockerels, as he told her how he'd bought his first motorbike on his sixteenth birthday and had come here for his first ride, solitary and free, the wind in his face—back then you didn't have to wear a helmet—and fast, like Speedy Gonzales, because his mother had told him his whole life that this was a place for crazies—but he didn't agree.

'I don't think they're crazy, these people, I think they just don't like how things are for them and they want to find a solution.'

Opposite them, on the other side of the water, Monique had returned to the shore. Standing on the beach, she stretched out one fat arm and then the other and shook each leg. Then with a loud shriek she ran, fully dressed, into the sea. She tripped and fell, then got up, soaked, hysterical, almost in a trance, and ran back, furious, into the sea.

'It's the ritual of the seven waves,' said Driss when he saw Sarah's puzzled frown. 'They do it a lot, these women. You see how they don't want to do it, they're angry, it's like they're going to war. I like coming here because these people are rebels, they're fighting. You see?'

Sarah turned to look at Driss. She ran her eyes over his hands, his fingers with the nails bitten down to the quick, his nose, those eyes of thyme plunging into the water with the same energy as her mother, his lips chapped with cold; and maybe this wasn't slow, swirling wind, cellos, all the harps of Mexico, maybe it wasn't quite Sergio and time stopping still, but he had the same fight in him as she did, and that was really something.

24

'DRISS ISN'T GOING TO MARRY you either, you know.' On the back seat of the 205, Chirine was wolfing down a portion of nuggets with barbecue sauce. Occasionally she shot a glance out of the window, but there was no need—at three in the afternoon in the middle of Ramadan there wasn't anyone else in the McDonald's carpark on the Corniche.

'Hurry up, Lalla,' her driver sighed in Arabic. He lolled against the steering wheel, his cheek resting on his bent arm, tapping the dashboard to the rhythm of the Oum Kalthoum song that was playing on Medi 1.

'Two minutes,' said Chirine with her mouth full. Sarah, beside her, turned her back. She stuck her head out of the window, beneath the white sky that, just as every year around mid-March, looked like it was finally getting ready to rain. On the beach overlooked by the carpark she saw boys in tracksuits, their lolling, scrawny bodies, their feet digging languidly into the sand. She wanted Chirine to get a move on too.

'I'm done,' Chirine said, sucking up the last drops of her Coke through a straw. As the driver started the engine she rolled down the window and tossed the brown paper bag out of the car. About time, Sarah thought to herself. She was upset and she wanted to go home.

She'd forgotten, that was all, and she couldn't quite work out how she'd managed to forget. She simply knew there'd been so many things since that January kiss with Driss, so many things that she no longer had time to think properly. There was the Walkman, the baseball cap and, later on, the video cassette machine that Driss came over to set up in front of her astonished mother. 'He's classy, this one,' Monique had muttered with a wink. There were still a few more days of Ramadan to go, and every evening the coffee table was strewn with crumbs from the Bennis sweetmeats that Abdellah and his mother had greedily gobbled up. They congratulated her with their mouths full, '*Tbarkallah* Sarah for the little husband!' Then there were as many magazines as she wanted, a dress, jeans, a backpack, a scarf. There'd been so many different things to distract her and make her forget. The school timetable had been adjusted for Ramadan and she couldn't get her head round it; that didn't help. Nor did the bloody prayers for rain from morning till night for the last month and a half, old men in djellabas kneeling on the pavement taking up so much space and stopping her being able to think. There'd been trouble in the group as well: the week before, Chirine had told her she and Alain had split up and she wasn't speaking to him, so now they were sharing their friends, seeing them alternate evenings. And Yaya, the bastard, still wasn't back. Every day Sarah hoped she'd see him, and every day—at the pool café, on the pavement on Rue Al Kabir—her heart broke again for the hundredth time when he wasn't there.

'He must have gone to Tunisia,' said Haroun. 'He's never coming back.'

As she walked back to the lycée after eating her pizza alone upstairs at the pool café, she imagined him smiling among the orange and lemon trees, applauding the sound of the guitar, watching girls' twirling skirts, happy at last, and she wondered if he'd ever know about the baseball cap, the sweetmeats, the Café Campus and all the rest, if he'd be proud of her, if he'd say, 'Bravo, petite, you've done good.' The Walkman, the school timetable, Chirine, Yaya, so many things confusing her, not to mention Driss every evening after iftar, the blurry outline she tried to trace, his Giorgio Armani cologne, Mille Bornes, those eyes like never-ending hills.

So many things, but even so, forgetting was going a bit far. Yet when Chirine began talking on the way to McDonald's Sarah had to admit the obvious: she'd forgotten about money. No one forgets about money like that, and Driss talked of nothing else, Driss who never talked. It was his language— even when he didn't say anything, it still spoke through him. Not just because of the Rolex and the huge house with the araucaria tree, the pool, the Rolls Royce in the garage; but because she could see that everything in his life was shaped by money—exactly as it was in her life. That was when she understood they were brother and sister. All Driss's comings and goings were about money—just like her; his movements were all about money—just like her. Even his thoughts, even his fits of anger, were all about money. When Driss finished school, his father sent him to France, Badr told her. 'He set him up nicely. The works,' he said. His father gave him an apartment to live in, paid for him to go to business school and sent him thirty thousand dirhams a month. 'He told everyone he sent Driss thirty thousand dirhams a month, he was very insistent it was thirty thousand, he went on and on about it: "Thirty thousand dirhams, thirty thousand dirhams a month."' Thirty thousand dirhams was the maximum amount a person was legally permitted to take out of Morocco a year, so when he told people it was thirty thousand a month it certainly had the desired effect, especially since on top of that there was the five per cent paid to the courier who carried out the currency exchange for him. And then, after a year, once the whole of Anfa knew about the apartment and the thirty thousand a month, and no one doubted the rumours anymore—he was as rich as the king, after all—his father made him come back to Casa. He wasn't going to keep up the performance for five years.

Three days after his return, Driss started work at Jean's Fabric. In the large factory in Sidi Moumen, even though business was booming, Driss still carried the battle over money deep in his heart. 'You've no idea how to make money,' his father told him as he signed yet another contract with a European business or came back from a trade fair with yet more samples from famous brands, while Driss had stayed behind in Casa to supervise the workers. Then one evening at

Badr's place last summer he'd seen an old friend from school who'd married an American and was working in New York, and he went for it. He'd already worked out what he was going to say—he'd gone over it a thousand times in his head, mumbling to imaginary Saudi princes and English business-men; and now at last, in Badr's garden, a joint between his fingers, he decided this was his moment. He said the words: 'Do you want to see my father's samples?' He'd been working for the company for four years, but he still didn't dare say 'our samples'. Anyway, a few weeks later he signed the contract— his first contract and Jean's Fabric's first American deal. He memorized down to the last detail the workings of the New York commercial port, and in November 1993 he signed off on one of the biggest orders in the factory's history: three red shipping containers, each holding fifty thousand pairs of jeans. Three red containers were going to the other side of the Atlantic, and they were sent by him, it was his deal, his signature, and yes, this was the proof he could do it, he too could make money, like a real man, like his father. All that was needed now was for the fucking client to pay up. Every day Driss faxed him a reminder. And when he got overheated, when he talked about the New York port, the cargo, the der-rick that was like a crane, the forwarding agent who should have insisted on receiving a bank guarantee on receipt of the merchandise, yes, who should have fucking insisted on getting the money, he always ended up weeping and trembling on Sarah's shoulder. Inside their little house she stroked his hair and murmured, 'They'll pay up, it'll be all right.'

All Driss's questions were about money. Since his over-heating wore him out, he didn't ask them all the time, but Sarah knew that they were seething constantly in his mind. Sometimes they burst out of him. When he came to pick her up in Hay Mohammadi, he didn't even say hello when she opened the door. He just stood there, arms crossed, staring into space. But it wasn't empty space that the thyme of his irises saw, it was everything, the universe ablaze, myriad storms. He saw everything. When he was like this, it wasn't even worth trying to talk to him. She walked behind him to his motorbike, pausing whenever the duck gait ahead of her stopped. He seemed to be talking to himself, he scratched his head, shook it from side to side, sighed and winced. Then he set off again with his web-footed gait. Almost every evening on the grey sofa the question erupted, as if it had swelled up inside him so much on the way back to Anfa that his mouth could no longer contain it. 'How do they keep going even when they're ill?' By 'they' he meant the female workers. It was always about the women. He didn't understand. When he was supervising them at the factory during the day, he'd stare at the scars on the backs of the hands of the women who sewed and overstitched, at the still-bleeding wounds on their fingers. Some of them were only fourteen. He stared at their acne-covered skin, the white pustules poking out from the side of their veils, or at the older women's wrinkles, liver spots and bruises. But mostly he listened. The women liked it when the boss's son came to see them, because he didn't insult them or yell, he didn't yell at them to shut up and work.

He just sat there, deaf and dumb, on a metal chair, his mouth hanging open under his big nose, waiting for his father to summon him back to the sixth floor. They could chatter away without fear. Driss heard a young woman called Zhor with yellow buck teeth giggling as she told the others about her mother, who she swore had stolen a hundred dirhams out of Madame's handbag and had managed to make the family where she worked as a maid believe their son had done it. The other women laughed—serves them right, they said, so long as your mother bought herself something nice. Then there was Mina, whose eight-year-old son had stopped going to school. He was hanging out on the street now and she was terrified he'd end up using karkoubi. She'd begged Driss's father to take him on at the factory, but he didn't want to because the Europeans didn't like it when you put kids to work. Several times a day, for no obvious reason, she'd let the fabric go slack, slam her hand on the table and cry out, 'I wish those Europeans would drop dead!' The other women were used to it. Then there was Najat, who'd got married in January, and her husband had forbidden her to carry on working. 'All day out of the house,' he complained, 'and with men in the building doing who knows what.' He couldn't bear it, so she quit. Two months later, he showed up at the factory with Najat in tow, muttering, 'I've brought her back.' Without her salary, they didn't have enough money to buy meat for Eid. So now every day while she worked, Najat griped about her husband, who spent his days lazing around and complaining she was disrespectful, complaining that now she'd gone back to her shitty job her housework had got sloppy. 'Who do you think you are?' he shouted at her. 'Just because you go out to work, it doesn't mean you're not a woman anymore.' Najat complained, but no one complained as much as Sanaa. She could read the numbers and letters on the labels in French better than anyone else—she still remembered her lessons from primary school—and everyone consulted her when they had to sew on a number for a size. But the fact that she could read so well changed nothing: every week it was her father who came and picked up her pay. She fantasized that one day she'd take the money herself, she said she deserved it, and she'd go and buy herself some nice clothes and a lipstick. Every single day she went on about this lipstick. The other girls listened, rolled their eyes, shrugged their shoulders and told her, 'Stop your nonsense, Sanaa.' They couldn't see how she was ever going to change the situation. 'God is great,' said old Hnia. 'Be patient, and one day, *insh'Allah*, you will find a husband, and your father won't be able to take your money from him.'

Driss didn't understand. Of course, he understood what they were saying, though their Arabic was better than his; what he didn't understand was poverty. Kamil had always understood it, and it had never bothered him. He'd hand two dirhams through the rolled down window to the attendant who'd kept an eye on his Porsche and made sure it didn't get keyed while he was having dinner at Boga Boga, and he'd say, 'May God protect you, my brother,' and the attendant would take the two dirhams and answer, 'May God protect you, my brother,' and then he'd drive off, and that was that. They both knew the truth: that was just how it was. But it wasn't possible for Driss, that that should be just how it was.

What did the women eat during iftar? Who paid their electricity bills? What were their homes like, how did they afford food, did they have a fan for the summer? What happened if one of them broke an arm? What did they do on Saturdays when they had the day off work? They couldn't even afford to go to the cinema with what they earned. No one in the whole world, from Paris to New York to Spain to England, was as foreign to Driss as these women.

Everything was about money for Driss; his language was money, and yet somehow Sarah had forgotten about money, had forgotten the subject of money. It had been a long time since she'd dreamt of the villa she would live in in Anfa Supérieur, filled with tiaras and diamonds scattered all over the floor. Her huge swimming pool the colour of the sky, the cognac in crystal glasses, the maids she would fire, her wedding in a caftan woven of golden thread, being borne aloft on brass trays to the sound of *darboukas*—she'd forgotten it all. Now their horizon was skin.

That was what she'd thought after Chirine spoke: that her horizon wasn't money now, it was skin, their skin, her skin was his skin, and his was hers. It didn't seem to mean much, said like that, but when you've spent your life walking the streets in your own skin, walking through bidonvilles and markets swarming with people, your fist clenched, ready to run or spit out an insult, and then from one day to the next you find yourself with a new skin constantly by your side, in the calm of a little house next to a rippling pool, a skin that doesn't speak, that plays Mille Bornes, that accepts you and asks for nothing and gives freely, you forget how to live like you used to in your skin of solitude, which isn't enough anymore. You forget how to put one foot in front of the other in the turbulent outside world. Just by being there beside her, every day, in silence, Driss had become the air, and he was also the ground on which she walked.

But then Chirine had said it, the fool. They'd left Driss at her house, the red house, negotiating for the zillionth time the price of her father's motorbike. They'd climbed into the back of the 205 and headed to the Corniche to eat nuggets in secret. On the way, Chirine launched into a furious tirade. She started going on again about the split with Alain, blaming him, saying how much she hated him, threatening to go to the very end of the Casa coast to see the love witch who everyone knew lived in the lighthouse at the tip of El Hank—she'd pay a hundred dirhams for her to cast a spell on the bastard or send a *jnoun* to his apartment.

'Never say such things, Lalla Chirine!' said her driver. But she didn't stop. She kept saying she couldn't believe he'd refused to marry her when she had tons more money than him, all because of some religious nonsense that could have been sorted in three months with the right rabbi. 'Fucking Jews,' she fulminated. 'Fucking boys, tempting us with the promise of marriage, then they dump us.' Sarah didn't say anything. She watched as they drove past the clubs overlooking the ocean, the Sun, the Tahiti Beach Club, the Miami, and thought to herself that once it was spring and Ramadan was over, she and Driss would go to one of those clubs and doze on a white wicker sunlounger, their skin stuck together, inseparable.

And then Chirine came out with it. 'They're all like that, the bastards, they're all the same,' she said. 'Driss isn't going marry you either, you know. I'm telling you straight, so you don't kid yourself and end up like me. He won't marry you. He'd never marry a girl like you.'

25

U PON ARRIVAL IN CASABLANCA, the second you walk
out of Casa-Voyageurs train station or the Mohammed
V airport, you almost get run over by some guy on a scooter
carrying a couple of sheep tied behind him on the saddle.
As you breathe in the humid air that stinks of iodine and
sulphur dioxide, you hear shouting, bleating, cars colliding
with vegetable carts; and you find out that in this place you
are dominated. You're dominated by the king, of course,
whose portrait adorns every grocery store and shop. And if
for some extraordinary reason you forget, then other people
will take on the task of reminding you. A woman stuck in
the back of her Jaguar in unmoving traffic winds down her
window and yells at a street kid hanging around on the pavement, 'Fetch me a bottle of water.' A cop grabs a girl by the
arm, hissing that he doesn't like how she's dressed, and the
girl begs, argues, weeps; the woman in the Jaguar sees her
and takes pity, lowering her window again and shouting at
the cop, 'Let her go.' And he does. When the woman gets
home, she goes into the house, inspects the couscous and

starts screaming at the maid, calling her a useless fool. She might even slap her. 'It's a disaster!' There's cinnamon in the couscous and her husband hates cinnamon, he'll be home soon, and the smell of cinnamon will make him angry. He'll shout and slam doors. In this villa, where his dominion is absolute—even more than his wife's over the maid, or the cop's over the girl downtown—there's panic. They'll have to make dinner again from scratch.

But there's one group that dominates all the rich men, husbands and bosses—the Fassi. They're called Fassi because they're descendants of old families from Fez, though few have ever set foot there. You can tell them by their bourgeois accents and their surnames. In the government, the Royal Palace, at the helm of major companies, they're all Fassi, exclusively Fassi; and if by chance a man from an ordinary family gains some kind of power, it's always less than a Fassi's power, for he, by the nobility of his lineage, holds the ultimate power. Being a Fassi is better than being rich. Fassi offspring become ministers and businessmen. But being a Fassi also means being rich, being rich for ever, generation after generation.

Nothing could be worse, as Sarah knew, than a Fassi diluting his blood by marrying a commoner.

Driss was a Fassi.

Of course, Chirine was right. A Fassi would never marry a girl like her, a girl whom no one knew anything about, and French into the bargain, who walked shamelessly in the street, a vagabond, not even a virgin, and no one had any idea what her father did. What Chirine had said in the back of the 205 was the truth, and those words had always been true, ever since the day Driss had opened his front door and led her into the garden, even before those eyes of thyme had met hers at a table in Café Campus. Sarah knew that, and perhaps she'd known it for a long time. But it wasn't the same once the words had been spoken—they blasted the air, split it in two. They hung there, flagrant, contemptuous, and if she turned her head, they mockingly followed her gaze. The fog in which she had blindly snuggled up with Driss through the whole of the month of Ramadan had dissipated, and now she could see. And now that she could see, it was the words she hated, their violence, more violent than men's blows behind closed doors, more violent than the poverty in the streets, than girls being raped in the bidonvilles, yes, more violent than all the aggression in this country that no one ever talked about. When Chirine had surprised her father with his hands on a weeping maid's arse, and told her mother about it, her mother had told her to hold her tongue: 'We don't talk about such things.' In this country, people understood better than anyone else in the world that the most devastating thing is not the thing itself, it's the words that speak of it.

The night after Chirine's words in the back of the 205, while Driss and Sarah were dabbling their toes in the icy pool beneath a dark, oppressive sky, listening, over the wind and the beginning of a storm—it was mid-March, at last—to the sound of each other's breathing, she asked him the question. She had never asked the question, not even when Driss was summoned from the villa's terrace at the top of the garden by a voice that was cracked from yelling so loudly, and he strode mournfully alone back up the lawn and then returned a few minutes later as if nothing was wrong. Because if she asked the question, she would have to say the words and there would be nothing left of their hazy equilibrium. But that night she asked him.

'Can we go up to the house?'

The sky rumbled. Earlier, on the 205's car radio, Sarah had heard a weather expert explain how, scientifically speaking, everything suggested that rain was imminent and would probably come in the next two days, because Ramadan would be over in two days and the rain would be a gift from God. 'Excellent analysis,' the journalist had replied.

Driss's feet stopped moving in the water. In a hoarse voice, he said, 'But my parents are there.'

Of course, Sarah could have made the effort to discuss it, to argue—she could have made rational points, such as Chirine's regular presence at the dinner table with his family, which didn't appear to bother him, the Saturday afternoon when, with his mother present, he and Badr had tried to install the new television in the living room, a huge black block, one metre square, so heavy the gardener had to call two of his cousins to carry it up the stairs. Everyone except her was always going round to his house. But there was no point pretending.

She drew her feet out of the cold water and calmly towelled them dry. Driss was still staring into the pool.

'But they'll be asleep.'

She noticed the very slight quivering of his nostril; she could imagine the wave of fear that shot through him at the thought of taking her up to the villa. He might be above the law, Driss the Fassi, as rich as the king, slipping hundred-dirham bank notes into policemen's pockets. But his sloping shoulders and duck-like gait revealed another truth—that he was weighed down by invisible chains lashed to his back attached to three red shipping containers, each filled with fifty thousand pairs of jeans.

Sarah took his hand. It was as cold as the bars of his prison, and her flesh shivered, and she thought for the first time that of the two of them, in this kingdom of the dominated, even if he had the same war inside him as she did, driving his motorbike to Sidi Abderrahmane to admire the non-conformists and the dissenters, she was the one—maybe the only one in the whole country—not simply to carry it, this war, but to wage it.

'Come on,' she said, getting to her feet and tugging him by the hand. 'Let's go up there.'

They walked through the garden up to the house, through darkened reception rooms with crystal chandeliers, bumping into a desk and a silk-covered footstool and stifling their giggles. Then they froze, afraid they'd made too much noise. Even though the master bedroom was on the other side of the house, they were nervous when they began to move again, hand in hand, across the dining room, past the four terraces, his father's study, Driss's blue bedroom with its mural of waves and boats. At the slightest sound they stopped. It was as if there were eyes all around them—behind the paintings, nestled in the keyholes of cabinets, beneath the cushions on the chaise longue, in the curve of the sofa. Sarah felt like there were a hundred pairs of eyes on her as she made her way through the rooms. She found the idea crazy at first, then she thought that, actually, you would need a lot of eyes to keep guard over the bottles of perfume in the bathroom that looked out onto Anfa Hill, to keep guard over the enormous vases of flowers, to keep guard over the carpets and carafes, to keep guard over the maids who slept in the basement and might make off with the jewellery. It wasn't as stupid as all that. And yet, even inhabited by all these eyes, as infused with fear as it was, as dark as it was—faintly illuminated by the light from the pool in the distance glimmering shyly through the French windows—Sarah thought the house was the most beautiful house in the whole world.

Now she remembered everything. All the money. She remembered all the paninis she'd eaten sitting opposite Driss, her dream wedding, borne aloft on brass platters, Marimar's dirty feet as she ran through Mexico after she'd stolen the oranges, Moustache's flyswatter and his tuna sandwiches, Loubna's tajines, her mother greedily devouring the pastries from Bennis. And when she caught sight of her reflection in the marble bathroom, she had no idea, she really didn't, what she had in common with the street girl she saw in the mirror. She belonged here.

They heard a sound from the stairs. Driss grabbed her arm, hurting her, and yanked her out of the bathroom, dragged her back down the hallway to the French windows. Panicking, he opened them and pushed her out onto the lawn. They ran down the sloping lawn to the pool.

'Hide,' he said, crouching behind a deckchair and looking towards the villa. He stayed like that, trembling at every rumble of thunder; but nothing moved up at the house. After a while, with a sigh of relief, he stood up. 'I think it was just the maid. I hope she didn't hear us.'

That was when Sarah realized there was only one solution.

26

THEY DIDN'T MAKE LOVE that often, but one day out of the blue she announced to him that she absolutely must not fall pregnant. Summoning all the urgency she was capable of, she told him he had to forge a prescription from Alain's father. He had to go to the chemist, hand over Alain's father's prescription, and say the words that she made him practise again and again: 'The pill. For my wife.' He hadn't blinked, hadn't trembled, he told her when he came out. The chemist hadn't asked him any questions—no one ever asked rich people questions. They were sitting upstairs at Crep'Crêpe and he reached under the table to hand Sarah a small green and white paper bag. Ramadan had just ended, it was raining at last and on television the king was making a speech about God and the brotherhood of man, all those who, for the last six weeks, had prayed in mosques, synagogues, the street—'Morocco walks hand in hand.' Sarah went home with the bag tucked inside her jacket; later that evening she threw it into one of the overflowing garbage bins behind the fence.

They made love every day now—he'd be stretched out on the pool table, taking a Rolex apart, or jotting down the weather forecast, and she'd come and lie alongside him. He'd look at her, eyes wide—'What are you doing?'

She hadn't intended to tell anyone about her plan, of course; but she told Yaya. A few days after Ramadan ended she was walking past Jus Ziraoui on her way to meet Driss at Café Campus, just as she used to, holding her new umbrella over her head, when she saw him squatting on the pavement, a joint between his lips, as if he'd never been away. That's what he said when she leapt into his arms: 'You're mad, I've never been away.' That same evening they met on the beach to watch the rain, where she told him about the weeks she'd been with Driss—the money, the baseball cap, Mille Bornes, the pastries, everything—and he told her about his brother, about the sea where he'd died, about those fuckers the Benchekrouns. She hadn't planned to tell him she wanted to get pregnant, and she probably wouldn't have done if they'd said goodbye after the beach and gone back to their own lives, him dealing drugs to the group, her hanging off Driss's arm at La Notte, or Badr's house, or 17 Storeys. But Yaya had the taxi that evening so he drove her home. Sitting in traffic on the Corniche, he started talking about the Benchekrouns again. 'I should have smashed their faces in. I'll never let a rich bastard call the shots again, no way.' Sarah sat in the passenger seat, her cheek against the cold window, and listened to him jabbering away; when she wiped away the condensation with the flat of her hand, the *jabane* seller appeared through the glass, sheltering beneath the statue of Sindibad. He was shivering; raindrops dripped from his rod of nougat. Yaya said, 'Fuck that bastard Benchekroun, I know what he does. I've kept my mouth shut all this time, but now I'm going to tell, I'm going to tell everybody what he does, that fucker, and he'll be sorry he never paid me for the gear.'

'What does he do?' asked Sarah, still staring at the *jabane* seller. 'You know what he does,' Yaya said, braking sharply. The other cars began to sound their horns and Sarah bumped her cheek against the window and turned towards him, annoyed, ready to spit out an insult; but seeing him shifting the gearstick without a word, his eyes on the road, she held back. Yaya's bony face—usually in constant motion, open-mouthed and laughing, teeth showing, spitting, loudly inhaling smoke or singing songs from Sidi Bou Saïd—was tight and still. His features had fallen, as though a second away from collapsing, one by one—nose, jaw, cheek, eyebrows—and shattering like glass on the car mat. He looked like he was about to cry. Sarah didn't dare say no, she didn't know what he was talking about, she didn't know what he did, that Benchekroun bastard. Yaya said, 'Even if I do the same thing as Benchekroun, at least I don't do it here, under the eye of Allah and my dead brother, in the middle of Ramadan; at least I know to get out of here. Every fucking Ramadan I get in the car and drive to Ceuta and I stay there the whole month so as not to soil my country with my sins, out of respect. He doesn't give a damn; he carries on doing his perverted shit while other people are fasting.

I'm going to tell everyone what he does. I'm going to say it, I don't care.' And as he turned onto Boulevard Moulay Ismaïl, where there weren't many cars and at last he could pick up speed, he added, 'When I was a kid, I thought I was the only homosexual in the world.' That was why she told him—because she also felt like the only person in the world. She didn't know any other girls of sixteen who sold off their bellies like her, making babies to change the course of their miserable lives. Yaya laughed. 'Stop talking nonsense. You're far from alone, petite.'

He was right. She didn't get her period in April. She was lying there in the living room, trying to sleep, thinking about it, the blue light from the television flickering on her eyelids, when she heard banging, like someone was trying to break down the door. 'Open up, bitch,' a man shouted in French. Sarah opened her eyes. She craned her neck to see out of the window; it took her a few moments to make out the furious face of one of her mother's old men from the Cercle.

Her mother took ages to get him to leave. She came into the living room in a yellow dressing gown—the dressing gown was short and you could see the varicose veins on her calves—and stood at the window, shouting louder than him, and waving her arms about. 'I don't have your fucking jewellery I'm telling you. I don't have it.' When the man began kicking, Sarah pushed the sofa against the door to block it. 'I'm calling the police,' Monique yelled, and the old man yelled back, 'Go ahead, call the police, they'll cut off both your hands, you disgusting thief, they'll send you to Inezgane, with the radicals and the gays.' Eventually, at dawn, he calmed down; everyone always calms down at dawn, because that's when other people start to stir and they know they're visible. In Cannes, Fat Joe never touched a drop during the day, but he really loved a beer after the sun went down and late into the night. 'But never in a bar instead of going to work,' he'd say to Monique, 'I'm no alcoholic.'

'All that for three shitty necklaces I pinched from his wife,' scoffed Monique after the old man had gone. The sun was up now, and she was standing by the kitchen sink, massive in her yellow dressing gown, holding a big bottle of Sidi Ali—every week Driss brought them a six-pack.

'What did you do with the necklaces?' Sarah asked, yawning. She'd lain back down on the sofa. She couldn't be bothered to shove it back in place and she could feel a cold draught on her cheeks coming through the gap around the door. She liked it; it felt like being on Driss's motorbike when he was doing a ton along the Corniche after La Notte.

'Sold them,' said Monique. 'She must have at least fifty, who cares.'

Sarah closed her eyes. She hugged the sofa cushions, listening to her mother noisily swigging greedy gulps of Sidi Ali. She heard her close the bottle, open the fridge, sniff. And then she heard her say that it was pretty rich, the old guy's bitch of a wife got pregnant with their kid on the sly, and he'd had to give her the necklaces so he didn't seem like such a fool, anyway one necklace more or less didn't make a difference, eh, and it was only fair because when she'd done the same thing to Sarah's father the soldier, handsome as Marlon Brando, he'd shipped out, the son of a bitch, as soon as he heard she was pregnant, he'd done a runner and she'd never got so much as a whiff of a necklace.

27

MAY WAS THE MONTH when the Sun began to get busy again.

It was packed until the end of October. Women lay sunbathing around the three swimming pools, their big, oiled bottoms spread over deckchairs that left rectangular imprints on their buttocks when they stood up to smack their boisterous children who were divebombing into the pool. 'Do your job,' they shouted at the paunchy lifeguard who was smoking a cigarette, before lying down again, their gold bracelets tinkling. Others ate fried fish with their husbands in the club restaurant whose terrace overlooked the public beach, while kids from the bidonvilles gave them the finger on the other side of the plate glass windows. Some of them, hysterical with laughter, threw sand then ran away. There were young people playing tennis on the Sun's clay court too, old men snoozing in the shade of the beach huts, cleaners kneeling between the sunloungers and wiping up puddles of spilt Hawaiian Tropic, waiters in white shirts soaked with sweat. It was a scene Sarah had imagined a hundred times whenever she walked past the entrance or tried to slip in behind someone and was chased away by a security guard, or when she clambered over the gate at night, carrying her sandals past the empty pools.

Now she was on Driss's guest list. Driss, Badr, Alain, Chirine and she had five reserved deckchairs and were ordering beer. 'Damn, I said I was giving up drinking,' groaned Badr when he saw the bottles. He'd managed not to let a drop past his lips the whole of Ramadan, and now he said he felt closer to God.

'Change religion, buddy,' said Alain, taking a swig. Chirine sighed. After Ramadan and the reopening of La Notte, she'd spent several nights at Alain's apartment in Gauthier. It wasn't like she had anything else to do, she told Sarah.

'You can do it, Badr, don't give in,' Sarah said, with an encouraging pat on his sweaty back. The bottle she was holding was open, but she hadn't taken a sip.

Every day since the pregnancy test she'd bought in secret from the pharmacy near the mosque and done at lunchbreak in the girls toilets at school, she'd been desperate to tell Driss. But she knew she mustn't yet—she still remembered the strange episode that had taken place in the bidonville two years before. A girl had been repudiated by her husband because she kept losing the babies she was carrying. Her pregnancies never lasted more than a few weeks, and one day her husband threw her out, screaming that she was cursed. After Abdellah's mother saw the poor girl returning to the bidonville, scarlet with shame, it was all she could talk about. From morning to night she kept on: 'The shame, that poor girl, repudiated like that, such humiliation.' Sometimes she shrugged and said, 'But you know what? She deserves it.' But the truth was everyone felt sorry for the petite, because she was a *bent nass*, a daughter of the people, who'd worn a scarf covering her hair ever since she was a child, never spent time with boys and lowered her eyes whenever a man spoke to her. She wasn't particularly pretty, and she spent most of her time at home. The neighbourhood women congratulated her mother for this excellent education and no one had been in any doubt that she would soon find a husband. And indeed, all it took was to send her to pick up milk from a grocery store in the centre of town for a man to stop her: 'Where do you live?' he asked. 'What's your father's name?' One week later he came to ask for her hand. The women in the bidonville ululated until sundown.

So when two years after the wedding the old women saw she was back, watched her dejectedly hanging up her parents' laundry, they couldn't help murmuring, 'What a tragic fate.' There was no hope for her now; she was past her sell-by date. Yet just a few months later, news spread that a man had agreed to marry her. He was a guy from Hay Mohammadi who didn't have a job, but he was a godsend for a divorcée. Lo and behold, nine months after the wedding she gave birth to twins. No one dared say it out loud, because they liked the *bent nass*, and no one wanted to be responsible for a second divorce, but the gossip spread all the way to Derb Sultan: it had to be witchcraft. Lots of people claimed to have seen her leaving Sidi Abderrahmane, and others said they'd smelt burning sage and wild rue outside her front door. People watched her kids—there was a third one after the twins—and couldn't help noticing that their eyes were brighter than those of the other children. Some local mothers wouldn't let their kids near them, they said they were evil spirits—'*Jnoun!*' they hissed between their teeth. Sarah didn't believe any of it, these stories of spells and child demons, but one evening Abdellah told her this: the *bent nass* swore she had nothing to do with witchcraft in public, but the fact was, once a week a group of women gathered outside her front door while her husband slept, where she whispered to them the spells she'd learnt—the ones that had kept her children alive. Some of them were common knowledge: jumping over hot coals, drinking rainwater while saying a prayer, sacrificing a cockerel of course, and not telling anyone about being pregnant, not a soul, for at least the first three months, to avoid the evil eye. Sarah didn't have coals or a cockerel, and it hadn't rained for weeks, but at least she hadn't said a word to Driss.

In any case he wouldn't have listened. They were at the Sun Club. While Badr sat at a low table, legs spread wide, peeling shrimps and loudly sucking the heads, Chirine was leaning against Alain and sharing music with him on her Walkman, and Sarah perched on the edge of a sunlounger eating a piece of watermelon and spitting the pips out one by one at some kids in front of her who looked around, bewildered, every time they felt the tiny projectiles hit their skin, Driss sat biting his nails. He hadn't stopped biting his nails for the whole three hours they'd been there, all while looking constantly at his watch—he was working out what time it was in New York, he said. Sarah put her head in his lap and could hear him muttering repeatedly, 'Three containers, fifty thousand pairs of jeans in each.' The client still hadn't paid. It was Labour Day in Casa, the weather was beautiful and everyone, even the women, was outside—but at two p.m. Driss was going to drive over to Jean's Fabric.

'Two o'clock here is nine in the morning in New York,' he said. At nine on the dot I'm calling. I'm going to call all day, every day, they'll have to answer the phone.'

They all tried to dissuade him, to get him to enjoy the day off, he could make the call tomorrow, but he refused to budge. At ten to two he leapt up, put on his flip-flops and tee shirt and hurried out of the Sun. 'See you later,' he called to Sarah, who lay down on the sunlounger and got out her Walkman. Inside it was the cassette the black-market guy from Derb Ghallef had made for her of all Madonna's songs, just as she'd asked, and some others by bands nobody had heard of. 'It's an exclusive, Lalla, just for you,' he'd said.

She summoned a waiter with a wave. 'Yes, Lalla?' he smiled as he reached her. Holding her headphones away from her ears, Sarah said in a clear voice, 'Bring me a bottle of water.'

The baby in her belly was already making her dizzy, when she stood up too fast or was sick in the morning. But what made her most dizzy was the lights, the hundreds of lights that would be hers after Driss married her, spinning above her head, like the twirling dresses she would wear, and the swirling patterns on the silken rugs, and the wooden spoon in the tajine, whose slow, circular movement lifted out the beef, the thyme and the bay. Madonna was singing in her ears as she cast sidelong glances at Chirine kissing Alain's neck, the gullible fool, kissing him even though he was never going to marry her. One evening, in the little house by the pool, Driss had told her that Alain was making plans to leave. He'd contacted an agency that organized immigration to Israel; he told Driss it wouldn't be long before there was nothing left for Jews in Casa, he had to find a wife, and if he stayed here he'd die of his addiction to karkoubi. Chirine didn't know yet. She just needed to fall pregnant too, Sarah thought, instead of being taken for a fool.

She had no idea if she'd fallen asleep for several hours or a few minutes, American pop in her ears. Suddenly she was jerked awake. A hand was shaking her, hysterically; and over the laughter of the kids in the pool and her own laughter in her dream, in which she was wearing a ballgown and her red baseball cap and dancing on a rooftop in Dar Bouazza, she heard a voice sobbing and repeating over and over again, 'At auction, at auction.'

She sat bolt upright: she'd never seen Driss's eyes like that. They were melting. They were detached, flowing onto the damp tiled floor of the Sun, and their thyme green held all the suffering of the Atlas, the screams of children falling from the top of the mountains. 'Calm down,' she kept saying, pressing her hands firmly on his shoulders. She could feel her headphones coiled in her long hair, the dangling Walkman tugging at the roots, but she didn't take her hands off Driss's shoulders. He was convulsing.

'At auction, at auction,' he kept saying, his eyes engorged with water that burst out and poured down his cheeks, the Ouzoud waterfalls on his face of rocks and craters, the Ouzoud waterfalls on his face that was the whole world. 'At auction, at auction,' he kept saying, and she kept saying, 'Calm down, Driss, calm down,' and she wiped his cheek with one hand, keeping the other tight on his shoulder because she knew if she let go he would die.

It wasn't until that evening that Sarah found out what had happened. The second time Driss called his client in New York a woman answered, the secretary. 'I speak to ze manager,' Driss stammered, kicking the leg of the varnished wooden desk on the sixth floor of the deserted factory in Sidi Moumen. He'd called the old schoolfriend who'd got him the contract with the client a hundred times since November. 'Don't worry, brother,' his friend said, 'they haven't had time to pick up the cargo from the port, it'll be a few more weeks, I promise. Next month, I promise, next month they'll pick up the jeans and you'll have your money.' So Driss waited. But the next month the jeans still hadn't left the port, no one had paid, and his father was growing impatient—'Where's the fucking money, Driss? Where is it?' And more weeks passed and his friend stopped answering the phone. So Driss began calling the company directly. 'I'm afraid the boss isn't available,' the secretary said every time he managed to explain in English what he wanted. When he grew angry, she said, 'Send him a letter,' and hung up. This drove him crazy. And then at last, months and months after the three containers each holding fifty thousand pairs of jeans had arrived at the port after thirty days on the sea from Casablanca, after screaming at the forwarding agent, the port authority, after fits of weeping against Sarah's breast in the little house by the pool, the secretary said, 'The boss? Sure, I'll put you through.'

Perhaps the boss was sitting at the very top of a glass tower looking out over the port of New York and smoking a cigar when he said the words. Perhaps he was dreamily watching the derrick as it dived into the fog, seizing one of the containers like a giant's arm. Perhaps he missed the November winds that brought cool fresh air. Perhaps he was sparing a thought for the port agent down below, sweating in his yellow jacket. Perhaps he had just turned on the air conditioning with a nonchalant flick of the remote control.

At any rate, that's how Driss pictured him when he heard him say, 'What are you talking about? We've already paid.'

The company had indeed, ten days earlier, paid less than a third of the price he had negotiated in November for fifty thousand pairs of jeans, the largest order in the history of Jean's Fabric, and their first American deal. For, as Driss discovered, trembling, as he clutched the white receiver of the telephone that sat on his father's desk, according to the rules of the commercial port of New York, all merchandise that remains uncollected after six months is sold at auction. The client had obtained the jeans he had ordered at the reserve price.

'At last you've figured it out,' his father laughed when Driss called, stammering with fury, to tell him the news.

'You mean you knew?'

'Of course I knew, you imbecile, and you can thank me for letting you do it, that's the way you learn in this business.'

And over his son's indignant splutters, he added, 'Relax, don't worry about it. It wasn't even that big an order.'

Sarah eventually managed to get Driss to lie down on a deckchair and drink some water. 'I'll order a taxi,' she said, 'and we'll go back to your house.' He didn't want to.

'I never want to see my father again, that son of a bitch.'

They lay there alongside each other. The others got up to leave.

'Will you be okay?' they murmured with worried expressions, their rolled-up beach towels under their arms.

'We'll be fine,' said Sarah, stroking Driss's forehead. They stayed there till sunset, eyes closed, listening to the sound of the sea, the tapping of women's sandals, the waiters expectorating as they leaned over the guardrail and looked down at the beach, holding glasses of tea. Every so often Driss gave a sudden start and began moaning again; each time Sarah placed her hand on his shoulder, and he calmed down. After everyone else had gone, as night began to fall, the security guard hauled his heavy body between the stacked deckchairs and asked them to leave. They went and picked up the bike. They didn't know where to go, so they drove to Hay Mohammadi.

28

WHEN SARAH AND HER MOTHER first arrived in Casablanca, they lived in a house in the Oasis neighbourhood. Didier found it for them. 'A whole house for the three of us,' her mother told her. 'And it's cheaper than Fat Joe's lousy flat in Cannes. Two bedrooms! A step up from sharing crazy Rita's sofa.' They were ten minutes from the Cercle Amical des Français. The last tenant had planted a rose bush in the garden, with flowers that looked like lipsticked mouths; when Didier and her mother fought, Sarah went outside to talk to them. She squeezed the petals between her fingers and let go and the lips formed words.

Then Didier ran off with the money that was meant for their shop, all Monique's savings, the loan in her name from the BMCI, and they never saw him again. The red mouths on the rose bush carried on chattering while Monique did the rounds of Casa, to beg the landlord to let her off that month's rent, to beg the school for textbooks and lunch in the canteen, to beg the people at the Cercle Amical for a job as a secretary or cleaner. She began going out at night, cheeks rouged, to hit the poker clubs. After her mother left the house in the evening, Sarah would go out into the little garden and listen to the roses whispering in her ear. She'd wait out there for her mother to come home. Sometimes she dozed off, and her hair got tangled in the twigs and thorns. She'd be startled awake by the sound of a car drawing up, and would tiptoe back inside; her mother would come in a few seconds later with a man or sometimes even two.

Then one day the rose mouths fell silent. Monique packed their suitcases. An old man in a Mercedes was waiting for them outside. He drove them to Hay Mohammadi, near the Carrières Centrales. On the way he said, 'You can just pay for water and electricity, that'll do me fine,' and her mother said, 'Thank you, thank you.'

There were no roses in Hay Mohammadi, and Sarah stopped talking. This turned out to be good timing, because Abdellah didn't shut up from the first evening he saw her sitting alone on the front step of their tumbledown house, waiting for her mother to come home. 'You can't stay out here at night,' he told her. He wasn't even ten. A little shrimp of a thing, he squatted on the railings wearing a football strip that went down to his knees and chewing one of the Flash Wondermint gums he hadn't managed to sell. His skin was still blemish-free. 'You're out here,' said Sarah. 'Yes, but I'm a boy.'

He showed her everything. Once, when they were crossing the patch of wasteland that served as a pitch, one of the football players yelled out, 'What's that whore doing here?'

Some of the other players, sharing a joint, cackled with laughter; some said nothing, just listened to the crunch of the empty can of Fanta they were rolling back and forth beneath their feet. 'Don't worry about them,' Abdellah muttered, so they kept on walking, ignoring the wolf whistles. The boys from Hay Mohammadi never stopped whistling when she walked by, even years later. But the thing was, they never touched her, which wasn't the case in other places; thanks to Abdellah they knew she was French, and French girls walked in the street, that was just how it was. Plus they knew that if they did anything to her, the French police would come down on them like a ton of bricks and they'd be sentenced to death, no questions asked. This meant that most of them didn't dare go anywhere near her. But they never stopped whistling.

She explained all this to Driss one night after he drove her home from the Sun Club. He parked the bike by the local school and they walked the rest of the way, past the market, dark and silent at that time of night, the pavement strewn with bright pink empty pots of Raïbi Jamila yoghurt, orange peel and mint leaves that had been crushed underfoot. Sarah talked and talked. She didn't stop. 'Did you notice before, when we drove past the empty lot, how the boys didn't whistle? When I'm with Abdellah or Yaya they whistle, but when I'm with you they don't. They're afraid of rich people.' She could have spent her whole life distracting him like that, keeping him from thinking about the dirty trick his father had played on him. She carried on talking almost without taking a breath, her slightly hysterical voice echoing among the silent tin shacks of the bidonville behind them. The second she stopped talking, Driss's eyes filled with tears again and his chest was wracked with sobs, and the Ouzoud waterfalls, the terrible Ouzoud waterfalls, looked as though they were about to spill over again.

'At auction,' he mumbled if there was even a split second of silence.

'No,' said Sarah, clasping his arm firmly. 'Don't think about that bastard, don't think about him, listen to me.' She pulled him along, telling him about the cops, who were worse than his father, way worse: once right here, in the market, she was just hanging out, she hadn't even stolen anything, but they picked her up anyway. 'Call that an outfit, with your shoulders bare?' one said, touching those bare shoulders, and when she pulled away he threatened to take her down to the station for being insolent. She'd run like crazy all the way to the old Saada Cinema; if you knew its secret corners, it was the best place to hide from the police. It was where karkoubi dealers did business and a few local guys brought prostitutes, slipping into the rows of seats in this place where thirty years before—back when a ticket cost only fifty centimes and people would elbow each other out of the way to get in—films were once screened. Proper films, according to Abdellah's mother, Hollywood films, with blonde-haired women and men in suits; sometimes, she said quietly, they didn't even cut the kissing scenes.

'Really?' Driss said with a snotty sob.

'I swear.'

'Rue du Lotissement,' she said. 'You see over there? That's the Derb Moulay Cherif police station; it's been closed the whole time I've lived her.' She said that when she used to hang out with Abdellah when she was a kid, crazy old ladies would scream at them, 'Get away from here, you little brats, it's haunted!' They'd swing their arms around and the wide arms of their djellabas would make them look like bats. Outside the police station Abdellah would pretend to laugh, but he was putting it on; inside he was dying of fright. Sarah didn't dare tell him what she'd heard one of her mother's wrinkly old boyfriends say—that it was the place where they tortured the king's opponents.

They walked and walked. She told Driss stories all the way to her house. She told him about the young boys who turned tricks at the far end of the empty lot, their clients the same men who spat at Yaya and yelled he was a dirty faggot when he drove past in his taxi. There was the girl who was raped in the street in the middle of the day; when her parents found out, they organized an ecclesiastical council in the neighbourhood. They didn't know what else to do to save their honour now she wasn't a virgin anymore. If the cops found out, she'd be sent to prison. It wasn't like it was for rich people here, you couldn't just get a hymen reconstructed whenever you wanted. Eventually the rapist agreed to marry the girl and everyone was very relieved.

Driss listened, horrified. It was like when he eavesdropped on the conversations between the women workers at the factory.

He was always trying to comprehend the strange ways of the poor, and Sarah was fully aware that the more she told him about Hay—its untrammelled violence, the way the cops bullied the desperate poor, always on the wrong side of the law whatever they did—the more Hay must have seemed like another planet to him. When Driss frowned and his mouth fell open, Sarah knew he wasn't thinking about the auction anymore. She kissed him on the cheek. 'There'll be other deals in America, you know.' He smiled faintly and then she told him about the kids who sniffed glue and the street hawkers.

They reached the house and sat down on the front step. Sarah threw a glance over the fence where years ago Abdellah had first spoken to her. The bins were overflowing. She couldn't take her eyes off them. She couldn't talk anymore. 'Are you okay?' Driss asked. Sarah stared at the Merendina and Skittles wrappers flapping around bits of broken plastic chairs, banana skins, gnawed cobs of corn, dirty nappies. Flies buzzed about the rubbish, even in the dark. It was in one of these bins the year before that someone had found a baby, its eyes half closed, smaller than a bottle of Sidi Ali. It wasn't crying. 'It must have been an unmarried girl,' the cop had said. 'Someone must have shopped her.'

'What the matter?' Driss asked.

Sarah looked at him. 'You're acting all weird,' said Driss. 'You're acting weird, I can see it, you're acting weird, tell me, what's the matter, why are you acting so weird? Tell me, tell me.' He cupped her sorrowful face in his hands and looked deep into her eyes, and she felt the cold steel of his Rolex pressing into her jaw.

'Tell me,' he said again. So she did. Quietly, she told him the story of the baby in the bin. She told him about the child-mothers, the children who were turned in by the hospital just after they'd given birth, who left in handcuffs, or the ones who managed to flee, limping in pain, no idea where to hide their babies: they stuffed them in cupboards or bins, or left them outside the front door of some fancy house in Anfa Supérieur rolled up in a threadbare blanket. She told him she didn't want to go to prison, and she didn't want the baby in her belly to end up in a bin.

Driss stared at her, stunned, the thyme in his eyes moving, moving in the hot bubbling oil of the tajine.

'What?' he said. Sarah prayed with all her might that he would understand; he'd understood everything up until now, he'd known everything and loved everything, he'd been her only friend since the roses shaped like mouths; her brother.

Driss gently let go of her face. His startled eyes moved from her to the street, from the street to the fence and the overflowing bins. He saw the flapping Merendina and Skittles wrappers, the gnawed cobs of corn and dirty nappies, and a little way away he saw the tin shack where Abdellah slept at his mother's feet, and all the other shacks, and the whole bidonville, and in the distance the streets of Hay Mohammadi where boys in football strips smoked while their sixteen-year-old wives rocked their kids to sleep inside their apartments, and he saw cops and beggars and the muffled cries of those who dared to raise their voices when they were beaten up in fake police stations, and the pieceworkers in Sidi Moumen, and the whole of Casablanca.

'Okay,' he said.

29

THEY SAT ON THE FRONT STEP of her house in Hay Mohammadi and figured out a plan; they tweaked it a hundred times, simplified it, learned it by heart and repeated it to each other until four in the morning, each correcting the other's slightest slip.

'No,' said Driss, 'you've forgotten a step.' So Sarah would start again. Every so often, hearing the rustle of palm fronds behind them, or some laundry slipping off one of the wires suspended between the tin shacks, they fell silent, and Sarah's hand would reach for the doorknob. But no one ever appeared, and as night fell they smiled at each other, trembling with excited anticipation now they had it by heart, and went over their plan one more time.

When it was time for Driss to go, Sarah made him promise that once they'd carried out their plan they'd come back. They'd sit here, right here outside the house, just the two of them, in the middle of the night, making a noise and maybe even holding hands, and when the cops came and demanded an explanation, they wouldn't hide, and they wouldn't negotiate.

They wouldn't give them a hundred dirhams. They would calmly hand over their marriage documents. They just had to wait three more weeks. In three weeks, it would be almost seventy days since the end of Ramadan and Eid al-Adha would begin. Sarah always hated this time of year, because for three days the whole of Casablanca stank like an abattoir, there were sheep carcasses hanging from the ceiling of every garage in Hay Mohammadi, butchers walking through the streets, their overalls covered in blood, holding knives and shouting, 'Butcher!' and entrails on the ground she always slipped on. The whole thing repulsed her. But this year for three weeks she kept going back to the makeshift tent that had been erected near the school, where entire families queued to order their animals. She went up to look at the bleating sheep along with all the men and women leaning over the pens, haggling, trying to touch their woolly coats. 'How much for that one?' asked a guy in a guard's uniform. When he heard the price, he was outraged: 'But it's so small!' The shepherd was turning this way and that, looking indignant as he negotiated the price, quoting the Koran to justify its worth, or taking down a fat woman's delivery address that she was painstakingly dictating while a snivelling kid tugged at her djellaba. Sarah tapped him on the shoulder while he was in the middle of dealing with a customer.

'Do you know the exact date of the festival?' she asked. When he saw her there in the tent again, the shepherd looked up at the sky: 'Dammit, I've only told you a hundred times already, kid, it all depends on the moon. Are you planning to come back every day and ask me the same thing?' Of course she was. Every day she came back and asked him the same question, and every day she relished the same response.

Driss was just as impatient. Sometimes he picked her up after school and when he saw her, with the red baseball cap clamped to her head and headphones over her ears and a shiny new pair of sandals like the ones worn by the Anfa princesses waiting for their drivers, he grinned. She grinned back, and they stood there on the pavement with their secret, staring foolishly at each other as if they were the only people in the world. The Porsches honked at them to get out of the way—one time it was Kamil in his convertible, who threw them a filthy look. They didn't care; in two weeks, in one week, it would be Eid al-Adha and their plan would swing into action. They drove past the line of cars at a hundred kilometres an hour, through Aïn Diab, past the *chouay Americano* where five months before they'd kissed for the first time. They stopped outside houses in Oasis, Anfa Supérieur and Californie. 'Let's live there,' said Driss. 'No, let's buy that one.' And eventually they arrived at the little house by the pool, lay down on the green baize table and dreamed of afternoons with their baby by their own pool, on their own deckchairs.

'I'll show him, I'll show my father I don't need him,' said Driss, rolling the number 8 ball between his hands, 'I'll show him that from now on I'm also head of a family, my own family, and I don't give a fuck what he thinks. I won't be his son anymore, I'll be a father, a man, I'll go on business trips too, I won't stay behind in Casa like a loser supervising the pieceworkers, I'll go away and then I'll come back with presents for you and the baby, so many presents, and you'll be the happiest person in the world and you won't have to deal with any more scumbags wolf-whistling at you in the bidonville. I'm going to get you out of there, because I'll be head of the family, head of my own family.' Sarah kissed him on the neck. 'What presents will you bring me?'

On the day of Eid al-Adha, Driss's parents and grandparents, his uncles and aunts and their children, were going to gather around the pool for the sacrifice. Like every year, there would be half a dozen sheep—one per family, to be slaughtered by the head of each family. But this year, when the old Honda in which the sheep were to be delivered drew up outside the house at seven in the morning, Driss's father would find there was one too many. He'd be surprised, perhaps he'd argue, but finally, after questioning the delivery man, he'd realize it was Driss who'd ordered the extra sheep. 'Why the extra sheep?' he'd ask his son. And Driss would tell him—he'd asked a girl to marry him. Now he was a man. To prove it, he'd go and fetch his future wife and introduce her to the whole family, and he'd slit the sheep's throat himself, as the woman he loved and his bastard of a father looked on, and he wouldn't ask his father's permission this time, because now, and everyone was going to know it, he too was head of his very own family.

30

IN THE SMALL BATHROOM off the bedroom in Sarah and Monique's house, a rectangular mirror hung above the basin. Whenever she tried on a new pair of jeans given to her by some boy, Sarah had to stand on a stool to look at her hips encased in the thick fabric, section by section. To see the effect of the flare around her ankle, she'd have to raise one leg, losing her balance in the process. Most of the time she gave up and relied on the unflattering mirrors in the school toilets. But there was no school the day of Eid al-Adha, so she had to do up the ribbon of the yellow dress Driss had bought her, with her thighs flattened against the clammy ceramic sink. As she knotted it, she watched herself in the mirror sticking out her stomach and pulling it in again to see what she'd look like in a few weeks when the *Negafa*, who looked about a hundred years old, wound a pearl and crystal belt around one of her seven wedding caftans. Maybe the old woman would notice the slight swell of her belly, but she wouldn't say anything, she'd just pull the belt a little tighter to quash any doubts and clasp a heavy gold necklace around Sarah's neck.

Sarah rubbed some *aker fassi* on her mouth and cheeks then dipped a wooden stick into her mother's kohl and drew a line along the inside of her eyelid. Her eyes watered and reddened from the peppery mixture, but it didn't matter; she looked exactly like a Fassi bride-to-be. She took a pair of fake pearl earrings from her mother's jewellery box, put them on and left the house.

Now she was waiting for Driss on the doorstep. It was nine in the morning, but she could already smell blood and grilled meat. Behind the fence stood some kids with the sheep the families in the bidonville had clubbed together to buy; they were checking it over, daring each other to touch it, tiptoeing up close and then hurriedly drawing back if it bleated. Abdellah was leaning against the wall of his house, smoking his kif pipe and observing the scene. He nodded when he spotted Sarah waiting at the front door. '*Hayhay*, Lalla Sarah, off to your *hlel* are you?'

Usually when he made a snarky comment, Sarah flipped him the bird and told him to shut up. But not this time. He was right: she was as good as married now. This morning Driss had stood up to his father, and this afternoon he would seal his destiny and publicly announce their engagement, and neither his brute of a father nor his mother would be able to do anything about it. They'd celebrate the marriage of their only son for seven days and seven nights in a Marrakech palace, with a thousand guests, governors, ambassadors and minor members of the royal family. Tongues would wag, of course, around the tables laden with lamb and candied figs, and in between the oud players' melodies, guests would whisper to one another, 'She's poor and French—for a pure-blooded family, oh the indignity!' But throughout the festivities, Driss's parents would keep tight smiles on their faces, concealing behind the bustle, the roses, the decorations and the oriental dancers their son's rebellion, his assumption of power.

At ten past nine Driss drew up on his motorbike. Sarah leapt to her feet and ran towards him. 'How did it go? Did you tell them?' He took off his helmet; she saw his eyes were filled with anxiety, like when a game of Mille Bornes was particularly close.

'I did,' he said. 'But there's just a couple of things...'

The couple of things were that when the extra sheep had been discovered and Driss had declared to his father with his head defiantly high that it was he who'd ordered it and he who would slit its throat, his father had laughed.

'You know how to slaughter a sheep, do you?' he'd said, handing a banknote to the deliveryman. Without waiting for an answer, he'd called out the names of the gardener and the driver and told them to deal with the animals, then gone into the house. Driss, unprepared for this, followed him. He watched the white djellaba sweeping through the rooms ahead of him, glittering in the sunlight that flooded through the windows, then turning suddenly towards the kitchen.

'Make me a coffee,' his father said to the maid, who was sitting on the counter watching an episode of *Marimar*. 'Yes,

Sidi,' she said, jumping down. Then he was on his way again. Driss couldn't come up with the blistering words he needed to show he was serious about the sheep, and for that matter it wasn't just about the sheep, so he followed him all the way to the cosy living room on the other side of the villa with the massive new Panasonic television that Badr had helped set up a few months before. With an elaborate yawn, his father collapsed in a sprawl onto the Italian sofa where his mother, wearing a loose pink gandura, was lying with her head on a silk cushion. She was watching *Marimar* too.

The father picked up the remote and changed channel. 'Why are you following me around like this?' he said to Driss, who was standing by the door. Driss clenched his fists.

'I'm going to slaughter a sheep.'

At that moment the maid entered the room with a tray, almost knocking into Driss. She set the tray down on the coffee table and began to pour from a cafetière into a little glass with an embossed silver pattern. Suddenly the father slammed his hand on the table so hard that the maid, cowering, spilled some of the hot liquid. 'Idiot, you've only brought one glass when there are two of us,' he shouted. She flinched and tried to wipe up the coffee with the tea towel knotted on her apron. He gave her a kick and hissed, 'Get out of here.' She picked up the tray and left. 'Such incompetence,' he muttered as he took a sip of coffee.

'Papa,' said Driss. His father turned to him.

'What?'

'I'm going to slaughter a sheep.'

He was prepared to repeat it a hundred times until the bastard understood he was divorcing him. His father let out a brief chuckle, turned to his wife and tapped her on the shoulder.

'He wants to slaughter a sheep.'

Driss's mother lifted her head.

'What?'

'Driss wants to slaughter a sheep,' his father repeated.

She looked incredulously first at her son and then at her husband.

'Does he know how to slaughter a sheep?'

'Apparently.'

The mother lay back on the silk cushion.

'So let him slaughter a sheep.'

The maid came back in with two glasses. As she was pouring coffee into the first glass, Driss stamped his foot on the floor. His father apparently didn't hear so Driss picked up a vase from the sideboard and threw it to the ground, hoping it would shatter. It didn't break—it was made of wood. It just rolled dejectedly over to the maid's feet, whose slight body was still crouched over the coffee table pouring a second glass. Her arm was bent but completely still. Driss's mother sat up sharply and his father froze, like the maid's arm.

So Driss told them everything—he was going to marry a French girl, she'd be there soon, and he was going to slaughter the sheep in front of everyone to announce their engagement.

His mother burst out laughing. 'Come on, Driss, you're not serious. You aren't going to get married without our permission.'

Driss began to shout. 'I am serious! I am!' He stamped his foot again on the floor, how he wanted to break it! How he wanted the whole villa to collapse, to sweep away all the other villas on Anfa Hill until there was nothing left in Casa except the swimming pool and the little house under the big araucaria tree which he and Sarah had made their refuge.

'I've asked her to marry me and now I'm going to tell everyone.'

He saw his mother's expression harden into anger. She told him to stop making a scene, she had no idea what had got into him, but marriage is a serious subject, he couldn't marry just anybody, certainly when he came from a family like theirs, if he really wanted to get married he had to do things properly, find a girl from a good family and introduce the parents. 'A French girl!' she exclaimed. 'You want to bring a French girl into our family, descendants of the Prophet, in front of everyone, during Eid al-Adha. You must have lost your mind.'

'Don't listen to him,' said his father, turning up the volume on the television, 'he doesn't know what he's saying.'

So then Driss launched his ultimate weapon. 'She's pregnant.'

Suddenly his mother and father were on their feet facing him, his mother shaking him by the shoulder and saying over and over again, 'How many weeks, how many weeks, how many weeks?' She turned to her husband and said, 'Who can we ask for an abortion?' Driss howled, 'No, no! I'm going to marry her, and we're going to have a baby. I'm going to slaughter a sheep!' His mother began to cry. 'It's not enough that you bring shame upon us with a French girl, but you want to ruin Eid by making a scandal. After all I've done—the maids have peeled ten kilos of vegetables, spent the whole week making pastries. I'm utterly exhausted.'

Driss felt bad.

'How can you do this to your mother?' said his father with a sneer of disgust.

They talked for two whole hours, his mother threatening to die of grief, the father threatening to cancel Eid, so deep was his shame, Driss slamming the door, coming back in, sobbing, saying he was leaving home forever, until at last they reached a compromise. Driss wouldn't slaughter the sheep, he wouldn't announce his engagement, and he wouldn't ruin the festival. But Sarah would be present for the sacrifice. They agreed to meet her.

31

Butchers roamed the streets, long knives attached to their belts, from the centre of the city all the way to Hay Mohammadi on the outskirts. Every few metres they were flagged down by families surrounded by bleating sheep, crowded into garages that were open onto the street. Some of the beasts were already dead, hanging by their hooves from a steel joist, blood dripping to the ground, flowing onto the pavement and into the sewers. Butchers either disembowelled them right there, rinsing their organs with a hose, or dragged the sheep by the hooves up to the kitchen of an apartment, or hauled them into the elevator. It was mayhem, women ululating, children wailing, butchers and animals bellowing. So when at last Driss and Sarah turned onto Anfa Hill, where the streets were quiet and pretty and the dead sheep had been hidden from view behind hibiscus bushes and garden chairs, they both smiled with relief.

Driss was filled with nervous anticipation. As he wheeled his motorbike into the garage, he rattled through all the cars he'd seen parked in front of the house: 'My uncle's Porsche, my cousin's BMW, my grandfather's Mercedes, a Range Rover I don't recognize. Do you realize,' he said to Sarah, '*everyone's* going to be here?' She bent down in front of the rear-view mirror to check that her mouth was still red with *aker fassi*, baring her teeth to inspect them. She did realize that everyone was going to be there, and suddenly, with another five metres to the bottom of the great sloping lawn she'd walked down a thousand times, she wasn't happy about it at all. She felt sick to her stomach. The last time she'd had to please adults who were better than her was at the Cercle Amical des Français when she was a little girl; thanks to her mother picking men up in the toilets while their wives sat smoking cigarettes and watching their kids on ponies learning to ride, that hadn't gone so well. The women always gave a little moue of disdain when they saw Monique and Sarah hanging around by the tennis courts; one time Monique walked into the games room for a bridge tournament and one of the wives got up and spat in her face. 'Fucking whore, stirring up trouble, go home!' Ever since, Monique and Sarah had tried to avoid being seen too often. They skulked in the shadows of these respectable lives, occasionally popping in with a flutter of eyelashes to steal a man.

'Stop fussing, come on,' said Driss, placing his hand over the mirror so she couldn't see her reflection. 'You're beautiful, everyone says you are. And even if you were ugly, we'd still win. Not one member of the family has ever brought anyone home for Eid without being married, do you realize that? It's never happened! I'm telling you, my folks are scared, they're terrified we're going to make a scandal, now they've seen I'm a man. I don't even need to slaughter a sheep. I can bring home whoever I want during Eid, you'll see, whoever I want; that's what it means to be head of a family.' He stuck out his chest like a little prince and the thyme glowed deep in his eyes.

As they made their way down the garden path, she kept her eyes on the new leather sandals he'd bought her, watching them as they sank into the grass. It was better than looking straight ahead towards the pool area that heaved with bodies and noise, so loud you couldn't even hear the crackling of the araucaria tree's needles. It was Driss who'd pointed it out one evening during Ramadan: 'Listen to the crackling.' She couldn't hear the water either. In the vast silence of Sarah and Driss's nights the water was like the muffled chime of a bell that only those who knew how to listen, only those who knew, like them, how to hold back the mad dash of the world, could hear. But now the sound of the water was drowned out by the chatter of voices around the pool, the clink of trays, the guttural moaning of the sheep. Sarah's left sandal sank into the grass, then the right one struck a tile speckled with araucaria needles. She looked up—they'd arrived.

To the left of the pool was a circle of a dozen men lolling on deckchairs with their legs spread wide. Some were smoking cigars. To the right a dozen women stood holding little glasses of tea in their fuchsia-tipped fingers, toddlers clutching their legs. There was a long table covered with a white embroidered cloth and laden with honey-soaked pastries, silver teapots and jugs of kefir. Sarah couldn't make out the women's faces, partly because they were eclipsed by the reflection of the June sun glancing off the water, and partly because of the maids in constant motion around them, holding teapots and refilling glasses as soon as they saw them empty, rushing over to the group of men the moment they heard the last drop of black coffee being sipped, like dogs to their masters. Suddenly one of the women lifted her arm, disturbing the motes of dust floating in the sunlight, and called out, 'Driss!' They walked towards her.

The first thing Sarah noticed about Driss's aunts and cousins as she greeted them was that the women all had long hair tumbling in glossy waves over their gold-embroidered djellabas. They got it done by Momi, the Jewish hairdresser on the Rue des Landes. Some had hair coloured with henna, its earthy smell still strong, the red, like the clay walls of Marrakech, more or less vivid depending on how much white hair they had to cover. As she smiled back at the women, Sarah thought they looked like they bore on their heads the ochre ramparts of the Medina in the shadow of the Atlas Mountains, where storks swoop in the blistering sunshine. This was why you had to be rich.

Perhaps if she hadn't liked henna, the Atlas Mountains, storks and the limewashed walls of Marrakech so much, Sarah would have understood sooner. She wouldn't have let herself be so intoxicated by the mint in the glass the maid handed her with a vague gesture, a gesture she had dreamed of for so long that it seemed as if she'd seen it a thousand times, like a tribal dance that her body remembered. The women laughed, teased Driss, asked him for his news, and Sarah was lulled by the glint of the diamonds that moved with their hands—it was so nice to be among the rich. She was at home here, among these women who seemed so like her, enjoying a foretaste of her real future life. She didn't spot their smirks when Driss introduced her—'This is my French girlfriend'—or the way they smiled at her tangled hair, her naked fingers. She didn't notice their astonished, almost frightened eyes that avoided looking directly at her and the fake pearls in her ears. If she had seen and understood, she would have left; but, blinded by their jewellery, she saw nothing and understood nothing. That was what she thought later when she got home: only rich people understand these things. When Driss's mother—tall, red-haired, straight-backed, stiletto heels clicking the tiles—embraced her son, Sarah didn't see anything either. She simply plunged into the colour of the mother's djellaba—emerald, like her eyes, like the precious stones that adorned her hands. It didn't matter that the mother muttered only the briefest greeting, lips pinched, barely glancing at her; with her big glossy curls and green eyes she looked like Lamia El Solh, the wife of Prince Moulay Abdallah.

All of a sudden she cried out, 'Everyone's here! We can begin!' Ululations rang out from the women's side. Everyone got to their feet, leaving smouldering cigars, empty tea glasses and crumpled paper napkins holding crumbs of semolina and powdered sugar on the side of the pool. A maid was already on her knees cleaning up.

'Come on,' said Driss. 'Let's go.'

They followed everyone past the araucaria to a small, covered courtyard where, on normal days, laundry was washed and hung. A man, his shirt unbuttoned to reveal a deeply tanned torso, greeted Driss with a slap on the back.

'Hey, kid, how're you doing? Making lots of money, I hope!' He lifted his chin towards Sarah in a gesture of acknowledgement. She couldn't take her eyes off the silver chains around his neck. A man in a djellaba pushed past them towards the sheep. Sarah saw a black ink mark on the nape of his neck, like those on the foreheads of old women in Maarif hair salons.

'That's my father,' whispered Driss. 'He's still upset but I don't care.'

Sarah liked the courtyard. It smelt of Tide. Over to one side bright orange boxes of powdered detergent were piled up next to a drying rack folded away into four; it looked like the throne she used to dream of sitting on while her hair was being dyed with henna in the exact colour of the Tide boxes and brushed into waves by Mimo on the Rue des Landes, as she sat drinking mint tea and looking out over the city. And then gradually, her eyes still filled with storks and gold bracelets, she began to hear.

While everyone in the courtyard stood waiting for the sacrifice, a man next to Driss and Sarah began talking. He said an Apache had asked for his daughter's hand in marriage—that was what rich people sometimes called the Berbers: Apaches. 'A Berber,' he said, looking appalled. 'I have no idea where she even met him, to be honest, what with all the money

I spend to make sure she only goes to places for the right kind of people. The thing is, it's impossible to protect your children nowadays. I said to my daughter, if I hear one more time about some wretch lusting after you, I'm confiscating the keys to your Jaguar. She cried, but I was firm: you can't be too careful these days.'

Driss glanced at Sarah and took her hand. 'Don't listen,' he whispered. But Sarah listened.

'When you start accepting people like that into the family,' the man went on, 'you end up with the whole tribe using your name and living off your coattails. Until one day at some ministry, before you know it, you find you're waiting in line while they've gone straight through. The world turned upside down, if you can believe it.'

There was a burst of heart-rending bleating. The man fell silent. Driss's father came round the araucaria, towing a sheep by its horns.

'It's time for the sacrifice,' Driss whispered to Sarah. The sheep was protesting, dragging its hooves, but it allowed itself to be hauled into the courtyard.

'Why doesn't it run away?' wondered Sarah.

Driss shrugged. 'Maybe it doesn't know there's a way out.'

Three of the guests went over to give the father a hand. Together they laid the beast on its back. It groaned when it found itself on the stone floor with its hooves in the air. The father raised a knife to the sky. With a swift, sure movement that cleaved gracefully through the air, he slit its throat. There were cries of joy.

The operation was repeated on each of the sheep tied to the araucaria. One by one they were slaughtered by the head of each family. The puddle of blood on the ground spread so rapidly that the women stepped backwards for fear it would touch their shoes. Two of the maids tried to mop it up. The butcher, the gardener and the driver pulled the dead sheep to the side then hung each one by its feet from a solid branch of one of the small yucca trees. Beneath its exuberant sword-shaped leaves, the animals dripped blood into pink plastic basins brought over by more maids. No one paid them any attention; but as an elderly uncle was completing the final sacrifice, Driss's mother summoned the houseboys who were busy hanging the dead animals. The men froze at the sound of their names.

'Come along, hurry up,' she said, clapping her hands. She pointed at the last sheep, which was still tied to the araucaria, and with a knowing look announced to the assembled company: 'We ordered it for the staff.' Everyone was delighted by such generosity. The servants made the last sacrifice and the guests wandered back to the pool. Bracelets tinkled, light from diamonds glinted off the crystal glasses. Sarah might have remained dazzled by it all, have held on to the glow in her eyes. But as she watched them—perhaps it was because the sun had moved, was no longer reflected on the water in the same way, or perhaps because of what the man had said—Sarah saw not only the uncles' and cousins' Rolexes, but also the noses that they were sniffing and picking, the burps that lodged in their throats beneath their silver chains, the way they proudly belched; she saw the lipstick moving on the women's mouths as they ran their tongues over their teeth, the way they howled like hyenas at their children and discreetly spat their semolina cake out on the ground so they wouldn't get fat.

She suddenly saw them with such clarity, while they weren't even aware of the sheep hanging from the yucca trees a few metres away from them, they were so focused on one another. They didn't see that the butcher had taken down one of the beasts and laid it on a bath towel; kneeling, he made an incision near the hoof then moved up to the head and bent right over it. He clamped his mouth and began to blow with all his might, making a few more cuts with his knife and blowing again, so that the skin peeled away from the muscle with the force of his breath, and after five minutes the sheep was completely swollen all over, monstrous. He began to chop it up. On the grass, near the hibiscus and roses, not far from the fountain and the pool, where the unseeing guests were asking for oranges, lay great chunks of raw flesh, muscle and bone, soon to be hacked into smaller pieces, the organs placed into buckets that wheezing maids carried one by one into the little house.

'When I was a child, I didn't want them to die,' said Driss, observing the scene alongside her. In the courtyard a puddle of pale pink blood diluted with running water was disappearing down the drain. 'I used to howl for it to stop.'

'And now?' said Sarah.

The last bucket was filled.

'I don't know anymore,' he said. 'It's become normal. So many things seem normal once you get tired of screaming.'

As they left the courtyard, they saw the driver lugging hunks of skin in a massive bucket. Sarah stared at them, then felt someone's fingers tapping her shoulder. 'Will you come and help me prepare the meat?' Driss's mother held the long butcher's knife between her painted nails.

32

S ARAH HAD NEVER SPENT much time in the kitchen of the little house. Driss went in there to fetch cans of Pom's. Sometimes when he fell asleep on the sofa in the evening during Ramadan, she'd wander in out of boredom, open the fridge, take out a jar of pickled cucumbers and eat them perched on a stool at the marble bar. She'd chomp enthusiastically with her mouth open, enjoying the sound of her teeth crunching in the thick silence of the night; maybe this time it would wake Driss. But nothing ever woke Driss, and nothing ever woke the kitchen either, which was as inert as the waiting room at the Mouqata'a where people like her and Yaya waited in the stifling heat for their certificates to be signed by the Caïd, who'd gone off for a siesta. People would go back to the Mouqata'a every day for a whole week for a birth certificate or a residence permit, practically melting in the sticky heat, to spend three or four hours squatting on the clammy floor alongside the old men and pregnant women sitting in the metal chairs. The only thing that cut short the Caïd's siesta was a hundred-dirham banknote.

But that day when she went into the kitchen with Driss's mother, the maids had brought it to life. Some were busy around the breakfast bar, carving up the bloodless animals. The pool table was covered with a massive wooden board on which sat several basins, and other maids were vigorously cleaning stomachs and intestines, plunging them into tubs of water while sweat dripped from their foreheads onto the knotted cord of their aprons.

Driss's mother pushed her way between two of them and shooed them away with her elbow.

'Give us some room,' she said. The older of the two looked at her, dumbfounded: 'Lalla, are you sure?'

'Of course I'm sure, Fatima, move!'

Having ousted the maids—they stood behind her, fretting—the mother took her place at the makeshift work surface, with Sarah at her side. In front of them, two sheep heads lay on their sides; they were charred but the dried blood from the decapitation was still visible at the edge of the neck, and the eyes were grey and glassy, shaped like March raindrops trickling down taxi windows. There were feet as well, the colour of ash, with still-pink hooves. Driss's mother took a deep breath. With one hand she grabbed a head and pulled it towards her, then tried, unsuccessfully, to slice one of the horns off with her knife.

'Pass me that little axe, Fatima,' she said. The maid sitting opposite her handed her the tool; the first then the second horn popped straight off. She handed the axe to Sarah. 'Your turn,' she said. 'I call them all Fatima,' she added with a little sigh. 'It's easier to remember.'

It wasn't very difficult to cut off the ears either, though she had to run the serrated saw over the cartilage several times. It was enough for Sarah to keep her inner eyes closed; she had to keep her real eyes open and alert, of course, so she didn't slice off a finger, but she knew she had to close her inner eyes, because if she didn't she'd see all the horror of the world, settled and accepted, and she would go mad.

'Now,' said the mother, 'you take this knife and carve off the top of the skull, like this.' Sarah reproduced the gestures one by one, quietly waiting for the questions or threats that might be brewing within this tall woman, her skin the colour of the walls, the traps that might be lying in wait. They scooped out the brains with a spoon. The maids carried on busily passing the washed entrails from hand to hand, the livers, kidneys, hearts and tongues, carrying them to the back of the little house to grill them—the smell of cooked meat was beginning to reach them in waves of smoke. The mother spoke.

'How pregnant are you?'

Sarah's hand slipped. She'd been about to plunge a whole brain into a bowl filled with water and vinegar, and now the gluey mass slithered from her fingers and liquid splattered the work surface.

'Two months,' she said, almost inaudibly.

Red and white cloths were already wiping up the spilt vinegar. Sarah didn't quite dare raise her eyes and didn't want to lower them; she kept them riveted on the bloody filaments of the brains floating amid the busy hands.

'I see,' said the mother.

With her long knife, she worked the cheeks from the sheep's head lengthwise, then handed the knife to Sarah.

'So you don't want an abortion?'

On the other side of the table, one of the Fatimas recoiled in shock. '*Allah yahafdek*,' she muttered beneath her breath, a look of horror on her face.

'No,' said Sarah.

It was her turn to begin slowly separating the ear from the head; she could feel the mother's emerald gaze sweeping over her, burning like the grill outside.

'*Hamdoullah*,' exclaimed the mother after a pause. 'It's a wonderful thing to keep it.'

Sarah looked up; her mother-in-law was smiling at her. Everything about her was smiling, even the gold-embroidered caftan and the precious stones and diamonds.

'It's a wonderful thing,' she repeated. 'Frankly, when I think about it, there were quite a few women who seduced my husband and fell pregnant, poor things. His employees, mostly. They saw me, they were jealous, so they decided they wanted to give him a child. Obviously we always offered to pay for an abortion as a favour, a gesture of generosity, really, but there were four or five who refused. Refused! I can't imagine what they thought. That my husband was going to give them money, or a house, or something like that. You never know with poor people. Anyway, may Allah protect them, he sent them back where they came from. They found themselves living in some bidonville with a babe in arms, not a centime to their names, the threat of prison hanging over them, the police knocking at their door every day, no food. What was so strange was that they knew perfectly well who they were. I mean, let's be honest: all this'—she indicated the maids with a movement of her chin—'isn't for girls like them. I don't know what got into their heads. They could have hung on as the mistress of a rich man, enjoying their gifts, and instead they got themselves into this nightmare. It's unbelievable, no? I shan't lie to you; I think about them sometimes.' Staring into space with a dreamy expression, she pulled open the sheep's jaw with both hands and tore it in two. 'Anyway, *tbarkallah*, bravo for your courage. It's not easy to contend with all that.'

She put down the pieces of the head and gently placed a bloody hand on Sarah's shoulder.

'I don't know what Driss has decided, but if he wants to marry you and leave the family home, I'm sure you understand we will not be able to help you. We shall have to remove him from the factory until he repudiates you and abandons the child. Perhaps he'll be able to move into your neighbourhood? You can find an inexpensive *ngafate* to marry you in the caves behind Hay Hassani, with a perfectly decent caterer, or so my gardener, the young one, tells me. Anyway, you must do what you want. I'm terribly sensitive, so it breaks my heart to see my son in such a predicament, but sometimes you have to go through something like this to make your children see reason. It actually happens rather often, sadly. Thank God, eventually they do, and they come back, and no one ever mentions it again.'

She wiped her hands on the teacloth that hung from the apron of the girl on her right.

'Anyway, if you change your mind about the baby, call me, I'll be happy to help. You have the number, *yak*?'

And with that she left, leaving Sarah with the mutilated sheep's head, and the horrified maids staring at her. It was hard not to cry, with that damn smoke from the grilling meat stinging her eyes. There was the clatter of knives, and the laughter from outside, and the people who were better than her who didn't look her in the eye, and the decapitated sheep on the green baize table where she and Driss had made love, their dead eyes like drops of rain, the stink of their guts, and the baby in her own guts, the baby that would eventually be born, and then it would be her who took her kid to sleep on crazy Rita the clairvoyant's sofa, maybe she'd end up the fat whore from Hay Mohammadi.

'There, there,' said the maid at her side, stroking her back.

'Fetch her a glass of water,' said her neighbour, and led her over to one of the grey sofas. She hovered nearby while Sarah gulped down the Sidi Ali, then looked up and saw Driss through the window, sitting shyly with the men and coughing every time he inhaled the cigar smoke. At one point he sat up straight, his chest out, and the second after, as if shot through with a shiver of anxiety, his shoulders dropped, like that night when he'd sat drinking a mint cordial all alone on a banquette at La Notte.

'It's okay, little one, it's okay,' the maid kept saying as she stroked Sarah's hair. She told her she shouldn't cry—frankly, she wasn't missing out on anything. She'd jumped for joy when she'd been hired by this family, she said, thinking it would be the end of her misery. Before that she'd been sleeping on the kitchen floor of a family in the Maarif who didn't even pay her, and the other maid was raped one night by the son lying right next to her on the floor. 'I was so scared my teeth were chattering. But it's no better here, you know, it's the same everywhere. You think we're better off here because they're rich? The father shouts louder than the men where I live in Hay Hassani, he beats his wife if she so much as scratches the car, and watch out anyone who wants to follow a different path to the one they want. They used to beat Driss with a belt when he was little because he wanted to watch *Marimar* with me and help me pod peas. Honestly, it's the same here as anywhere else in this country; there's always someone there to dominate you. Domination—I swear, you'd think it was the national language. If I was in your place, if I had a passport, I'd jump on a plane and go to France. Over there they say everyone is equal. Can you imagine? People are equal there.'

33

A BOY ONCE TOLD HER that in other places, far away, the sand was velvety soft, white as clouds; he talked of seashells and the smell of salt, the music of the waves. She didn't believe him.

'Stop with your bullshit,' she said.

'But it's true, I swear on my mother's life it's true,' he insisted. 'The sand there is like flour. My cousin told me. He's been to America.'

'Oh, shut your mouth,' said Sarah. She couldn't let him carry on saying these things. If what he said was true, it would be too much to bear—he must know, the idiot, that you can't change the sand you're born on.

Sitting on the grimy sand on Beach 56 writing in his notebook, Driss was even more of an idiot than the little boy from the Carrières and his tales of flour and America. He had to be to never once look up at her. It was as if they'd never stood side by side in the darkness of their little house drinking Pom's in silence. It was as if, with his eyes of thyme, his milky skin, his crooked nose and his Rolex, he'd never been a brother to her, with her terracotta skin and her homemade dress, her twin in fact; so precisely were they each other's opposites that for six months, stuck to each other's skin that had become their entire horizon, she'd been him and he'd been her.

'You fucking fool,' Sarah muttered through gritted teeth each time a wave crashed loudly enough to cover her whispered words.

Chirine had warned her when she arrived: Driss was sulking. If it had been up to him, he wouldn't have come to the beach with them at all. Alain had nagged him for hours, 'Come on, brother, do it for me, to say goodbye.' Alain was leaving. It was all sorted. He'd been through the whole process with the Jewish Agency, who'd paid for his flight to Israel—Alain, who'd never gone beyond Laayoune. 'Can you even imagine?' said Chirine. The week after Eid, he'd invited everyone to come and get stoned on Beach 56 for one last time; Yaya brought free kif for everyone and even a bit of karkoubi, even though for the last two months he'd shouted at whoever wanted to hear that he'd never deal it to Alain again—he couldn't bear to see his teeth falling out. 'It's OK,' he said, slipping the pouch of pills under Alain's beach towel. You won't find dope like this in Israel.'

Yaya was throwing stones into the Atlantic; he kept saying, 'You're right, man. You're right to be getting the hell out of this shithole.' Driss had begun a game of patience. Whether Sarah, a metre away from him, was lying on her stomach like an American starlet or not, he didn't give a damn.

He'd seen her weeping on the sofa in the little house on the day of Eid. It had lasted the briefest of moments; the moment when her bloodshot eyes caught sight of him sitting there with the men, an unlit cigar in his mouth. As he struck a match and raised it to his lips, he glanced through the window. Seeing the tears rolling down Sarah's face, he froze; the cigar drooped towards his chin, the match burnt between his thumb and his index finger, the undulating flame seeming to salute her. Behind the glass, hiccupping, she responded with a little wave.

'It's not going to work, you know it's not going to work,' she kept saying in the courtyard afterwards. She was leaning against the pile of Tide boxes, tracing dark lines with her sandal on the damp tiles that were still tinged with pink from the blood. Driss watched the movement of her foot. There was the smell of sheep guts and fake jasmine from the washing powder and they could hear the kids splashing as they jumped into the pool.

When she told him what his mother had said, he listened, horrified, panting loudly through his nose, faster and faster, like a cow that was about to die. Eventually he stammered, 'It doesn't matter, I can get a job.'

She shook her head. 'Yes, I will,' he said, filled with sudden courage. 'I'll call Alain, I can go into property. It's not difficult what he does, he'll teach me, and I'll earn money, and we'll find an apartment for the two of us, and we'll bring up our child.' Sarah shook her regal face. 'No,' she repeated.

'Okay,' he said, 'We'll start with an apartment, and then I'll buy you a house. I'll earn lots of money, all the money you want, and first we'll get an apartment, then we'll get a house, I promise you, we'll get a house.'

Sarah stared down into her lap. 'No,' she said again. Driss began to cry. 'I promise, I promise, a house, I promise, I promise I'll do it.' He was weeping like a madman. She kissed his wet cheeks, her lips stumbling over the craters of his skin with each sob. 'I promise, I promise,' he kept saying. She left a few moments later. He was moaning with grief, doubled over next to the boxes of Tide, and the waterfalls of Ouzoud were flooding over the tiles and, she thought as she ran towards the gate, perhaps soon they'd erase the drawings she'd done in the dirt with the new leather sandals he'd bought her.

They didn't see each other again. The next Monday Sarah walked for two hours from Hay Mohammadi to the lycée; by the time she got to the Casa-Voyageurs railway station the pavement was crowded as ever with boys on scooters, cigarettes between their lips, tooting their horns like crazy when a pedestrian got in their way. She had to weave in and out of the cars jammed on the road; there were cops in the middle of the intersection, sweating in their uniforms, cheeks flushed crimson, whistling frantically and waving their arms. When they saw her, they dropped the whistle they held between their teeth, and it was those yellow teeth that Sarah saw waving in front of her as they grinned at her, 'Oh, what's she doing there, the gazelle? Hey you, lost your way? Come here, don't be afraid.' The yellow teeth beneath the curl of their lips were as yellow as the field of sunflowers behind the Sindibad amusement park that she'd seen go by from the back of Driss's motorbike, but these sunflowers, these tartar teeth, didn't go by any faster than her sandals that were suddenly going faster, and when she felt the warm hand of a cop trying to grab her by the hips she began to run. 'Slut,' she heard him say as she raced panting down the Boulevard Mohammed V.

When she reached the lycée, she slumped down under a tree behind Building K to smoke the cigarette she'd bought from a kid in the street. In every corner of the school playground there were girls with hair straightened at the hairdresser and skin tanned from a weekend at the Sun or the Anfa golf club, dappled here and there with paler patches, between their collarbones from a gold pendant or on their wrists where they wore their Rolexes. Sarah stared at them, wide-eyed. Since she'd left Driss's house a few days earlier, since the moment she had gone out of the door and, for the second time that month, walked on her own in the empty streets of Anfa Supérieur, her eyes had felt wide and dry; she blinked slowly at the strangeness of the world, like someone short-sighted who has recently been fitted with glasses. He was no longer by her side.

'It's not him,' said Yaya, when she flinched at the sound of a motorbike. They were sitting on the pavement outside

Jus Ziraoui. She went to find Yaya every day, either there or at the pool café, where he'd be squatting on the pavement smoking, and she squatted down next to him. 'Why are you hanging around me like this, move,' he said; but she didn't move and he got used to it. She needed another skin, after spending six solid months glued to Driss, Driss who was her horizon, blocking out the rest of the world—just from time to time, to remember what it was like, even if Yaya smelt of tuna and that made her cry even harder.

'Oh, stop blubbering,' he snapped, shaking her hair away— she was sitting so close to him that one of her curls had got up his nose and made him sneeze. 'He's a good guy, Driss,' he said, wiping the snot from the palm of his hand onto the pavement, 'but that didn't mean you were going to end up with him. You're so pretty, you'll find another rich guy, maybe not as rich as him, but anything's better than struggling on your own with a kid in the middle of the city like everyone else. A house in the CIL, that would be okay, no? With your face, you'll definitely get a house there. You'd better invite me over.' It was Yaya who'd handed over the paperwork for the abortion at the Clinique des Camélias. He told her Driss had kicked up hell with his parents so they'd get her an appointment in a real clinic and not the bathroom of some quack they'd heard about who also happened to be a beautician in the Maarif. 'It costs a fortune at the clinic,' Yaya told her, 'ten thousand dirhams for them to make it look like it was appendicitis. There's almost zero chance of you dying there, which isn't bad when you think about it.' The appointment was for the following Monday, the day after Alain's leaving do at Beach 56.

After Beach 56, they said goodbye. Alain hugged them tightly, one by one, whispering in their ears with his tobacco-scented breath, 'I'm going to miss you, brother, how I'm going to miss you.' Chirine stood apart, looking at the sea so she didn't have to watch; bathed in the red rays of the setting sun, with her long hair, she looked like an Apache. Then they climbed into a taxi to Anfa Supérieur, all except Driss who went to pick up his motorbike in the parking lot behind McDonald's without so much as a backwards glance in her direction.

As night fell, she walked across Gauthier. When she reached the Place des Nations Unies, she turned towards Derb Omar. She walked through the fishing port. It stank of sardines. The fishermen were tying up their boats on the quay, still wearing their little white caps even though the sun had sunk behind the sea an hour before. Driss would never have been able to put up with the smell of sardines every day. He wouldn't have been able to put up with slipping on all the foil yoghurt pot lids that lined the pavements, or queuing at administrative buildings, all those people crowded behind glass, dying from the heat, while the son of some businessman who'd made a fortune in tinned corn jumped the queue, enthusiastically shaking the hand of some civil service employee. Maybe he'd have broken his leg in a motorbike accident and he'd have been sent to a public hospital to wait in a corridor with a dozen other patients, screaming because the health ministry didn't have the money to supply painkillers. He'd have worked and been robbed, as all the poor are robbed, and he would never have said anything; there's not much you can say to a rich man who had dinner the night before with the judge.

And he'd have gone crazy, like all the poor people of Casa go crazy, beating each other up out of despair, spitting on women in the street and dreaming of American sand; crazy like she was crazy to have fallen pregnant. But he didn't see all that. The truth about Driss was that up there on his hill, fixing his watches on a pool table in Anfa, he was the only rich person who didn't want to see the guerrilla warfare between masters and slaves that his father, his mother, Badr, Chirine and all the others adroitly preserved—they were even crazier than the crazies in the streets, hysterically afraid of anything that might destroy the stability of their kingdom. Badr had cackled when Driss, drunk at 17 Storeys after a night at La Notte, kept asking, again and again, why the boy who served them their quiches was just a twelve-year-old kid, why were his eyes always bloodshot, why didn't he go to school, and why did he sleep here on the floor of the bakery after the customers had all gone home to their villas in Anfa?

'But this is where he lives, you imbecile,' said Badr, and everyone laughed with mouths full of flaky pastry and cheese, and thought how bonkers he was, this Driss, the way he didn't understand a thing about how things worked. He was the last person not to have collapsed into the insanity of this place.

She reached the house. When he saw her from behind the fence, Abdellah greeted her with a few well-chosen epithets; even after she'd slammed the door behind her he carried on needling her, chanting obscene lyrics to a local song, changing some of the words slightly to incorporate her name. Usually she yelled back something even louder, they could cheerfully spend an hour flinging insults back and forth. But this time she turned up the volume on the television to drown out his voice. Anyway, all she could hear was the sand from Beach 56 that crackled in her hair as she coiled it nervously around her index finger and punctuated, grain by grain, the single thought going round and round in her head: tomorrow, at the Clinique des Camélias, it would all be over. Then, to the rhythm of her thoughts, of the grains of sand on Beach 56, of Abdellah's insults and the national anthem playing on 2M with a montage of Morocco's red flag waving in the wind, she cried again as she cried every day because she was going to have to live without him, even though she knew better than anyone that in this country you couldn't live a dignified, free life if you were poor. Driss thought it was true if you were rich as well—you weren't free and you weren't dignified if you had to bend like he had to bend to the violence of his masters. He said he'd have no regrets if he turned his back on them. But he didn't see the glaring truth: if you're going to be in chains, they may as well be gold-plated chains winding around your wrist.

He was the one who called her on the telephone as orange as a glass of Fanta that he'd fixed to the wall by the fridge a few weeks before. He'd explained that if anyone called her, it was free, and if she was the one who made the call he'd pay the bill. But Monique didn't understand how the people from Maroc Telecom would know who'd called who, she swore it was just a trick to fleece them, which was why she'd never wanted a phone in the house. She didn't give anybody the number. Sarah gave it to everyone, even to Yaya who always said you had to be a headcase to have a thing like that in your house—it could ring at any moment, he said, 'like that, no warning, don't you get it?' He stood for an hour a day by the telephone booth on Boulevard Zerktouni to receive his calls, and that suited him perfectly. Sarah wasn't allowed to call him at the phone booth, so as not to disturb him while he was working, but every so often he called her because he knew it made her happy. When she got home she'd sit down cross-legged on the floor by the fridge and wait for it to ring. Sometimes it was Yaya saying, 'There you go, I've called you on your damn phone. Happy now?' Sometimes it was Chirine, who would complain for so long about Alain that Monique would begin to yell, 'For fuck's sake, hang up, do you think we're the royal family or something?' But the best was when the phone didn't ring at all. Sarah liked to get up in the middle of the night to watch it while it slept, gleaming and orange on the peeling wall, holding all the voices in the world, all the way to America, linking them to her, and it was so new that it erased all the mould and the smell of the bins, and she lifted the neck of the bottle of Fanta to her open mouth.

The last words of the national anthem finished playing on the television—*Allah, Al Watan, Al Malik*, God, the Fatherland, the King—and there was a brief moment of silence just before the Sunday evening film; that was when the phone rang. '*Allô*?' she said, her voice husky. He spoke in a single breath. He didn't say, 'It's me, it's Driss,' he just said, 'It's tomorrow at ten, in case you've forgotten, you mustn't be late, it's Dr Bennani you need to ask for.'

'I remember,' she answered.

Then he said, 'If you like, I'll send my driver, but it'll be him who takes you, not me, and if you like he'll bring you home, but it'll be him who brings you home, not me, I'm doing something else, I've got something else on.'

'Okay,' she said.

'That's it,' he said.

Behind her on the television screen, the credits were rolling for an Egyptian film where women fainted and men were boxers, and then there was nothing. She said, 'We could go for a ride on your bike if you like.'

That's how it happened. He came to pick her up, just like before. She climbed onto the back of the bike. They drove down the Corniche, past Aïn Diab, the salt from the sea stung their cheeks, and then suddenly they were at Tamaris, and then even further south, driving towards the eucalyptus forests of Azemmour which smelt, with the wind, like his Giorgio Armani cologne. And then they were heading nowhere in particular, and he shouted in her ear, 'Look how free we are! We can do whatever we like.' In an hour they reached El Jadida. They drove through the fortified city, between the bastions and the ramparts, every so often coming across two or three kids playing football, faintly lit up by the moon. The bike had to go very slowly down the narrow streets, tiny within the immense fortress, and they couldn't find the way out, if there was one. They thought they could smell the sea more strongly on the right, so they followed the road that way, delighted to realize that the ground was getting wetter, which maybe meant the sea was nearby, but after a few metres they saw a high, rusty gate ahead, the waves crashing against it then fading away, which kept them stuck in the citadel. Driss said nothing; he turned round and made his way back through the maze of streets, and it was Sarah who whispered, 'We can't do whatever we want, you know.' He sniffed and hastily wiped his cheek with his hand. He said nothing, kept looking for the way out of the citadel, and she stroked his tear-stained face, the craters and dunes she knew by heart and on which with the tip of her finger she could trace the path she would have taken with him, her only friend, her brother, if there hadn't been so many walls surrounding him. Driss took a left and suddenly—victory, there was the way out, there was the endless road following the Atlantic.

They kept driving. One hour, maybe two, faster than any Rolex, Driss stopping to sob and then to negotiate—'Yes, we can do it, listen to me, I'm telling you, we'll be all right'—and she kissed his damp eyes that tasted of salty thyme, about to disappear, along with the beef tajines in villas with gilded walls, the weddings on brass trays, the tinted windows of Rolls Royces, far from cops and robbers. He snivelled, and they carried on driving.

In the middle of the night they stopped somewhere between Bedouzza and Safi, four hours south of Casa. The coast here was edged with high cliffs like you almost never see in Morocco, and they stayed there, at the top, sitting on the bike with their arms around each other like a king and a queen. They heard the waves breaking far below.

'I know you're right,' said Driss. His tears had dried, his hands were on the handlebars and he was staring at the dark water, the filthy water full of plastic bottles and the spectral corpses of the Benchekrouns' victims.

'Yes,' said Sarah; she held him tight, her head nestled into his shoulder and her terracotta skin stuck to his milky skin, just as it was meant to be. And then Driss said, 'You know, we could just keep going.'

'Keep going?' she said.

He didn't take his eyes off the horizon.

'Yeah, keep going, down there, into the water, into the Atlantic.'

He turned to look at her. 'Worst comes to the worst, we drown. But if we're lucky, we'll end up in America.'